About A Girl

Tony Nesca

<u>**By Tony Nesca**</u>

Stale Anchovy Kisses -

Dead Bats Amidst The Bullshit Laughter And The Lovestricken Cockroaches –

Hollow Man –

La Gioconda -

Charlie -

Mondo Cane -

Dishpig -

About A Girl -

Emma Strunk -

Jukebox Music -

La Gioconda (the novel) -

The Do-Nothing Boys -

Bulletproof Smile -

Vodka Orange Sunday -

Hobo –

Crazy Legs –

Junkyard Lucy -

Last Stop To Saskatoon

ISBN: 978-1-7752112-3-5

Published by Screamin' Skull Press

screamingskullpress.net/

Printed in the U.S.A.

What you are about to read is a work of fiction

Winter day at bus-stop hands in pockets puffing smoke thinking 'bout a bike I had as a kid in this very neighborhood, retarded boy named Ken used to challenge me to race wobbling from side to side as he rode making car sounds on that old fucking thing basket in front, "rooom roooom" "come on retard boy, that all you got?" racing down Garwood Avenue that crazy loon flying right by me up to corner then back and forth laughing like the world is all right and it's there just for us my mother on front porch shaking her fist at me "beep beep" goes Ken, I'm thinking about this at bus-stop mid-day streets alive with furious wanton music, young woman shows up out of the darkness "hello" lights cigarette, winter day gray and shady,

"So who are you?" she says as the lights go wiry,

"Uh-huh, oh yeah"

"I turned 23 yesterday"

Old lady walks by well-scrubbed pink tragic like the sun she smiles at us young woman beside me we're talking high-speed 'bout local bands booze on her breath I should be going home on call for work security guard at downtown high-rise she's smiling big black hair we're on the bus going through little Italy restaurants bars cafes go by in a blur I'm telling her I used to play guitar in a band her green eyes light up "should have known" she says,

"Why, cuz I got long hair?"

"Yes"

She pulls a mickey out of her knapsack takes a swig hands it to me I decline, think about it, then I take a sip bus racing through The Osborne Village artsy part of town funky shops black clothes mohawk kids begging for money guy with glasses throws up on corner,

"Where you goin'?" she says

I explain the work thing gotta sit by the phone in case they need me, got an hour to kill she's looking for CD's, likes That Petrol Emotion and The Violent Femmes, going to that second-hand music place downtown lady on bus starts singing Old Man River I laugh alive in love, my friend beside me laughs too applies deep red lip-stick snow piled high on the boulevard cruising down The Osborne Bridge sweating in our winter jackets bus cramped and tired nippin' vodka between the sheets my friend looking brave and thinking, she's reciting a Black Flag song whistling in the wind, howling at the septic tank says she used to live in Toronto hates it grew up on Indian Reserve called Pukatawagan says Winnipeg really works for her, really like The Peg she says, guy snoring behind us, bus-driver taking crazy turns announcing each corner with lame-ass joke crowd laughing like derelicts my friend looks at me crosses her eyes sticks her tongue out I feel my ass-cheeks rumble, damn...

"Ever been to The Canadian Shield?" she says,

"Oh yeah"

Gust of wind gives Cocker Spaniel on corner a mouth full of snow few guys on bus start laughing shiny hair suburban nightmares my friend comments on them doesn't like that type big fucking deal I say do you listen to Brave new Waves? Sure thing she says, new band called The White Stripes pretty good love that three chord unorthodox rock and roll...similar to what The Pixies did I say,

"No one's as good as The Pixies" she says

Approaching downtown the drunks come out middle of the afternoon stumbling through parking lots and construction sites she digs it says life is about this takes another sip of vodka I join her people on the bus take notice driver looking at us in mirror let's get off I say...heel-toe-express down the downtown streets chinese guy parking car reminds me of something I can't remember my friend exactly same height as me short parka with hood tight blue jeans beautiful winter I'm thinking breath comes out in clouds we live one step at a time caught in the shit of things stick and move monkey man on high wind tears out brain things as usual he says, business guy walking fast briefcase dangling I point to a mall then past it to a small bar hungover mohawk-kid in front wrapping his jacket around him lighting cigarette,

"Let's go there" I say,

"Juicy" she says

Crossing the street people lined up like tombstones woman laughing alone in storefront, car slides on ice tilting to one side then regains focus me and young friend skip by whistling some pirate idiocy she grabs my jacket from behind we do the alternative-rock-hurly-burly, I'm thinking of this young guy I used to know at University, young writer had a chapbook published we talked the writing talk during English lectures and over coffee, I think of his beautiful green eyes and vague suburban looks, you never had it buddy, that's all there is to it, door opens into smoky room smell of beer and maybe a touch of urine on Fort Street middle of the day,

"Two drafts" I say to the bartender old drinker

VLT's making sounds people gambling for that one last thing, long narrow bar booths hugging the walls place full of drinking laughing end-of-the-line types, my friend talking to one of them waving her hands one leg leaning forward my eyes follow the line of the thigh in those tight denims, the ass-cheeks reaching for the sky like a basketball in mid-motion, I reach her point to a booth we sit and smile drink and talk rebel and curse I'm looking at my watch thinking about work gotta get home soon my friend keeps talking,

"I remember this bar in Toronto where all the alternative bands played"

"What kind of bands?"

"Bourbon Tabernacle Choir, King Apparatus, Bob's Your Uncle, New Duncan Imperials..."

"Seen them all here at The Spectrum"

"Love The Spectrum...rock and roll isn't as dead as people think"

I think about that with a cigarette in one hand and a draft in the other looking around blue smoke curling to the ceiling at every table,

"Do you realize next week smoking in bars is gonna be banned?" she says,

"All the charm in the world disappearing one chunk at a time"

"Bars with no cigarettes..."

"Seems a bit insane, doesn't it?"

Having this sit-down with young broad from bus-stop full of electricity and territorial rock and roll obsessions chain-smoking in the gray dimness of an afternoon bar jaunt comparing guitar riffs from different records arguing at every turn I get lost in those deep red headlights without being pretentious, without any specific desire or belief, adrift in the cigarette butts and punk-rock ashtrays young fellow with shaved head asks for smoke I give him one as he walks away,

"See?" she says "you see?"

Sanctimonious little wench I'm thinking 'bout the space between the table and her crotch, huge black hair making shadows I have her undivided attention waving my hands distant crazy talking like the devil in chinos, one cigarette goes out another is lit she listens as well as she talks rare species this Indian beauty cutting me off describing Northern Manitoba living on The Rez wild immaculate,

"Wait" I say "wait"

"Your turn Ziggy"...

Long green carpet cigarette burns narrow place old bartender taking shots with the patrons fucking freezing outside misunderstood and hazy we order our second drink young goth types share a booth serious confused deep sorry amber reaching for drinks leather wristbands thinking sex and words and bullet holes...got no time or concern for the problems of the world, living pure and uncaring is what I want, not selfish but PURE, seemingly cold and distant but actually alive and understanding and unwilling to shut my eyes to true human nature, middle-aged waitress serving cheap draft in tall glasses gnarly fingers wrapped tight my friend slurping beer eyes laughing, says Elvis Costello is the real king of rock absolute expression on her face takes off parka wearing black turtleneck shows me a joint in her Du Maurier pack I nod she follows me out we're in back alley fire-escapes and broken bottles sirens in the distance puffing on joint sweet fire down my throat she punches my arm lightly starts coughing up a lung, I kick a pile of snow sun starting to rear its head through dark clouds, she takes my hand we turn the corner, light a smoke, throat burning, thirsty eyes watering, open door walk inside, our booth with full ashtray, half empty draft glasses, sit down my queen, let's continue...

"Don't like this hip-hop bullshit" she says "it's worse than that seventies shit"

"There was some good music in the seventies, if you can sift through that self-indulgent arena crap"

"Sorry but a twenty minute guitar solo with a violin bow doesn't do it for me"

"Like I said, skip that bullshit, listen to Alex Harvey and Lou Reed, guitar solos or not"

"You wanna buy some pot?"

"You got some?"

"That's what I do for a living, got a gram of black hash too"

Blast from the past comes up to me, tall black guy with dreads red eyes,

"Hey man!"

We do the street handshake, he takes a seat

"How goes it?" I say

"Just got in from Toronto...hate this fucking city"

"Why'd you come back?"

"Got caught with a gun...had to split"

"What's your beef with The Peg?"

"It's a fucking waste zone, nothing to do, no night-shit experience, no bitches here to fuck, no nothing"

I look at my friend no expression on her face guy continues,

"Was in the joint for awhile, no bullshit in there man, no bitches..."

"Still playing guitar?"

"Yeah, you?"

"Not professionally anymore, for fun"

"You should have never quit man, lotsa bitches in rock and roll...got any blow?"

"Don't do that shit..."

"What do you do?"

"Just pot and booze"

"And bitches" says my female friend

Guy starts eyeing her up and down always was dangerous type of freak, he's looking with x-ray gunshot eyes, she's looking back not a hint of fear or shame bold pouty lips teeth clenched in laughter guy walks away all street and hustle macho confusion full-of-shit-motherfucker bus-stop-girl starts talking again like he was never here got boyfriend back in Toronto but,

"It's not very good, not very good at all"

"It rarely is" I say "rarely under the sun and damn the laughter anyway"

"So where do you live?"

"By Central Park in a highrise"

"The one with the Mac's store attached to it, or the other one?"

"The Mac's store"

"Pretty rough neighborhood, got a girlfriend?"

"No, no, like I said, damn the laughter"

"I'm one hundred percent monogamous"

"That's a bit conservative, isn't it?"

"Conservative hell, how about you?"

"Maybe not one hundred percent, but monogamy really works for me..."

"Let's have a shot of Sambuca, ya dig?"

Couple of freaks sipping on Sambuca and cheap draft is what we are and always will be old fuck tired drunk stumbles past us orders whiskey shot other guy playing sport- select greasy hair parted on side, my friend crosses her legs touches my foot under table wave of sexual tension up my spine cigarettes mix with afternoon derision while waitress in baggy pants waves a hand and smiles at native couple in the corner, Filipino plugging the jukebox, white-man pacing up and down looking wired and electric, far in the back musician tunes his six-string, jazz in smoky room cliched and alive waiting on the job ain't no damn good, neither is sailing the seven seas sober and unhinged, she makes music singing without singing, doing without doing, wild day in the sunlight of afternoon barroom, she makes me crazy young beautiful left of normal, continue I say, continue,

"I don't mind jazz but I need some rock and roll right now, got a loony?"

I flip her one she glides to the juke in slow motion easy vibration full of curves and attitude black boots sliding across the cigarette butts almost clumsy, almost perfect, chinaman hogs space she motions him aside they laugh and talk she makes her selection CCR shaking her hips back to our table I get up, rotate, sit back down, cigarette between my fingers beer in hand mind confident shifting from this to that wave of energy slices across the room she's laughing loud and insane and wild and desperate and separate ideas with nowhere to go spin like death illusion strawberry vodka twist of ice Patty Smidtch down the turnstile,

"You're much more than a security guard" she says,

"I don't think so"

"Don't give me this modest bullshit"

"You can go fuck yourself"

"I like fucking myself, want another draft?"

"Yeah, sorry about the fucking yourself remark...I'm a writer"

"Anything published?"

"A novel, a few chapbooks, strictly underground...more to come"

"Here's to more to come"

"Cen't anni"

We hit glasses like regular drinking fools around the world more native guys come through the door beautiful long black hair old woman with cane follows trailing mud and snow from outside cook in stained white apron serving cheeseburger and fries and coleslaw -

"I know that cook" I say "jammed with him a couple of times at parties"

"Let me guess...he's a bass player"

"Drummer..."

"The hell with him"

Sadness of the world ain't nothing old fellow at the urinal shoots the shit with me, don't got the heart to tell him to fuck-off which is what I want to say but instead,

"Have a nice day buddy"

He walks away happy that someone took the time, I hear him shouting for a drink as the door closes and I zip up, look in the mirror thinking I'm losing a job today, walk out into the smoke and sallow faces, my friend smiling right at me like she was waiting for this moment her whole life,

"Looks like I'm losing my job today"

"I was wondering if that security guard thing was bullshit"

"No bullshit, and no point in going home now"

"Fuck it, it's just a job"

"Exactly"

Secretly worried about the fact I light another smoke, act like the whole thing means nothing in the grim light of living jukebox making funny sounds wondering where to go from here my friend with her cigarettes and abundant laughter argument in the corner meaning nothing to me, to her, to anyone with a belly-full of delight and desperation couple of drunks join us male and female used to drink with them at the dive down the street we're talking the good drinking talk serious then playful I'm telling stories everyone listening from one corner of the globe to the other everyone laughing while dying and living reaching for a smoke a touch of grace drunken woman hitting on me,

"I'm with her" I say,

They talk a bit more then hit the road we're alone again,

"What do you think about this war on terrorism thing?" she says,

"Don't give a damn"

"I support it, it's the first war I've ever supported"

"Would you go fight in the front lines?"

"Hell no"

"Then how can you support something you won't fight for?"

"You're being smart, that's what you're doing"

"I was hoping for a clever comeback, but I ain't got one"

"What is with you?"

"How do you mean?"

"Well, it's the way you talk, whenever you open your mouth people listen...in the last hour I've seen you talk to a punker, a gangster, a couple of drunks, and it's the same every time..."

"It just looks that way, it's not really like that"

"Ever been to Toronto?"

"The airport"

"You're not missing anything, it's fucked-up"

"I've heard it's a beautiful city, very alive and happening"

"It seems that way, like most big cities, actually it's anything BUT...I've traveled the world, I know"

"How did you manage that?"

"My old man was in the military...and when I grew up he was very generous with his money, and don't give me any spoiled-daddy's-girl bullshit"

"Not at all, I wish I was a spoiled-daddy's-girl"

"Funny guy...

"No, I mean it"

"I've seen all of Western Europe, China, spent a year in Tokyo, a few months in Australia"

"Sounds like a good time"

"A blast man...how about you, what have you seen?"

"Don't like to travel, but I'm from Italy, been back and forth several times, seen a bit more than I would have liked"

"Italy? Wait a second, you don't like to travel? How can someone not like to travel?"

"Hold your horses kitty kat, I'll tell you..."

We're interrupted by another one of my downtown drinking cronies, retired office-worker loose tie booze on his cheeks fell from grace at his job forced into early retirement questionable character always liked this guy with his status-quo rebellion we have a few laughs he moves on clock says mid-afternoon feeling the beer and the pot my friend's face flushed and happy Nirvana coming from the juke wasted afternoon in the urban Canadian prairies one more draft I say then let's, let's move on...

We cross Fort Street through wind and snow reach Winnipeg Square an underground mall enter down escalator office bustle suits and ties and skirts and high heels sex is everywhere bulging wallets and ambitions I show my friend the lottery booth I used to work at my boss an older fellow with cerebral palsy we formed a tight friendship loved the way he smiled, used to ride on the back of his electric wheelchair up and down the mall great buddies fucked-up in our ways and desires, my oldest friend was the janitor there also singer in our rock group cruising for chicks while pushing mop behind the suits leaning on wall talking waving his hands, down the street our practice hall old character building drunken caretaker always a party sex drugs and all the rest, fell in love here as they say, broken heart here as they also say, walking past the shops and food joints and the beautiful women of Winnipeg and the past happenings old friendly ghosts my friend walks clumsy leaning forward like her tits are too big, rolls up her sleeves tiny tattoo on forearm I can't make out fat guy in bookstore reading Hemingway, young woman checking out Tolkien, security guard pushing panhandler out the door, upscale lounge on the left chalkboard saying gin and tonics on special, let's go there I say...

Soft jazz in background the well-off leaning back sipping cocktails gin in my mouth down my throat thinking I would love to do this more often, to do nothing but hang-out with a cigarette between my lips maybe a drink in hand, waitress short and beautiful long blond hair chunky thighs whole thing perfectly organized like a gift from the gods, my friend laughs for no reason, for the fuck of it, for the sheer absolute bullshit of it all, long cool and graceful she's insane with laughter, rich couple looking at us like we're crap,

office worker sipping Manhattans on corner barstool
he's looking tired and married and trapped,

"Strange what people do to each other" says my
friend,

"How do you mean?"

"Well, they trap each other, don't they?"

"I suppose..."

"Why can't you have a completely equal
relationship?"

"I don't think it's possible given what we are...too self-
important on all levels, how else would you explain
religion?"

"So what are you, a guru of some kind?"

We laugh cuz it's funny, cuz I'm telling half-truths
about myself and she's digging it...under the dim light
of the world lighting cigs with a vengeance sense of gray
purpose madness and lost living, read book called
"Siddhartha" I tell her, already have she says,

"It inspired me to make the heaviest commitment I
will ever make"

"Yeah, what's that?"

"I promise (and she puts her fingers to her mouth
when she says this) to never do anything I don't want

to, to not waste one second, not one second on anything I deem as trivial or inconsequential, not a job, not a lover, not anything"

She sits back holds my eyes in place with extreme serious, then she smiles, then she laughs, I laugh too thinking this is some classy bullshit, the balls, the sheer audacity, arrogance confidence grim beauty, classical music comes out of tiny speakers on the ceiling mixing with quiet talk about nothing, it hovers over the tables then dissipates into the ceiling like the shit it is my friend and I talking loud and boisterous wasting time like death in the afternoon with ambivalent desire trippin' like hippies out of place and mind gray-haired couple to our right orders sushi "well done" laughs the old fellow "well done" somewhere in the room there's a british accent asian lady dancing slowly towards the bar red-head waitress lights cigarette takes off one shoe teenage busboy wired and nervous hating all this as he should girlfriend at home smoking pot my friend returns from washroom seems electric motion as her hips rotate left then right throws me a glance I lean back cool and easy man like wallflowers and butterflies and rat scurvy and guitar licks and gypsy rose racing down the alley slow-motion-girl sits across from me adjusts turtleneck I start talking she leans forward hands on chin listens intensely...

Last drink in the land of plenty we move forward and out the door up the stairs and out the front door, wind hits us hard but the booze holds it back late afternoon sun already starting to go down dim orange paints the streets jammed with end-of-the-day-work-types, my friend walks and I watch her black army boots make imprints in the snow,

"Is it getting warmer?" I say

Her parka hugs her waist fur collar black and white hangs over back of neck she walks heavy forward motion slightly humped over thick curly hair bouncing, smiling from here to there short bursts of laughter I see a doorway in a back alley suggest we smoke a joint crossing Graham and Fort Street we take a right huddle in doorway lighter takes several tries then the gods give us a break joint is lit we puff by a garbage bin young guy in kitchen whites comes out door garbage bag in hand brown stain on smock sees us I raise my hands, oh well, he joins in has a puff we clear the fuck out...everyone on the most basic level wants to have a good time, they wanna be-bop the night away rock and roll and slide guitars groove and shimmy until it's time to say goodnight...

Start heading right on Graham past the post office stoned red and blue shades of purple in our minds reach the library follow me I say and she does walk inside security guard old and angry wife at home tired and lazy, I offer him a piece of gum, he takes it uninterested uninspired lost in the fold, my friend moves quickly towards the poetry section I follow like a sexual deviant she's showing me Dorothy Parker, Gertrude Stein, Rimbaud, Alice Munro, talking endlessly on their merits (and demerits) something by Raymond Carver turns my eye I flip a page my friend watching I'm showing her bits and pieces of this great writer, she doesn't like it polite but obvious, don't like Mordecai Richler or Bukowski either she says, I seriously think about walking away there and then but ask her about Whitman instead, too American she says,

prefers European sensibilities, what about rock and roll
I say,

"Not only is that purely American, but it could never
have come out of anywhere BUT America"

"I'll give you that, I didn't mean to make this a
political issue" she says quiet-like

"How about we move on out of here" I take a step she
follows -

Past the books, the bums, the security guard lonely
young lass out of time and witless outside snow falling
in big flakes I watch my friend's wet curls getting
tighter as they roll down her shoulders, I'm waving my
hands shuffling along talking fast listening easy time
long-haired scruff that I am she glides rock and roll
violence takes my arm sticks her tongue out we're
moving in that same inevitable direction feels warmer
out here arm in hand down the cobblestone and ice
snow falling in big far-apart flakes Graham Avenue
lined with black streetlights banners with pictures of
old Winnipeg draping down the sides bum on every
corner coffee-shops bookstores pawn shops people
hanging out looking grim and dour we follow the mood
to an old hotel seedy bar called The Garry average age

60 only young guys talking loud and tough we sit at a table with two old ladies and a red-faced drunk laughing before I even sit down my friend's shaking hands large rectangle room no windows no music just a bunch of people getting drunk late-afternoon midget in corner talks in high-pitched voice fat guy with shades smiles continually young tough guys getting louder gray-haired lady selling herself fringe lunatic circles the bar eyes bulging bartender huge guy mid-fifties tattoo on forearm says "Mi Vida Loca" waitress Filipino woman nasty no bullshit complains about sore feet tells filthy man at center table to fuck himself I'm talking with old ladies one flirting crazy my friend making faces in the smoke-filled room we're insane, we're fringe-living, we know nothing....

People coming down from hotel in bathrobes and slippers white hair uncombed lonely years behind them time for the bottle and little else, there's a steady sound of merrymaking and a hint of violence, some leave for their rooms and a nap, others come down just getting up from the nap eager for that push towards death and final happiness "gimme a few drafts" he says, people I recognize talk with me, we shake hands, move on, sound the trumpets baby I'm coming on in!

Most just lonely and desperate not a bad way to end up I think, not so bad,

"Come with me" says my friend eyes smiling,

We say goodbye to our table I follow her to a corner we're standing one inch apart smoking cigarettes and laughing leaning against the wall painting of a loon on a lake some trees in background,

"So what happens now?" she says,

"One moment at a time"

"Think I can light a joint right here?"

"Don't think so, this isn't our world, we're just visitors, let's not thrash up the place"

"Visitor hell, if you weren't still young you'd fit right in"

"I've been coming here for years and-"

"-You call that a visitor?"

"And every time I walked through that door I was just dropping in, know what I mean?"

"Oddly enough, I think I do, oh fuck look at that..."

Tough guys crank it up punches are thrown one guy falls proceeds to get vicious beating kicks to the head everyone silent and watching tear in the universe thunder and darkness guy then picks up chair smashing limp body repeatedly blood spurts on wall the horror of all this numbing until I decide to move step in the middle immediately followed by a throng of drunks everyone suddenly brave and willing, we step between the bullshit start pulling bloodied guy up as we hold him other guy lands a punch through the confusion hits the jaw and I swear I hear something break, bartender has guy in full nelson cops are called ambulance arrives, scene clears out everyone starts talking about the incident immediately at the same time, we're bummed out, I look at my friend, she's looking down, smile gone she's humped over, I butt my cigarette on the filthy carpet, let's go man, let's split, she follows, I put my arm around her,

"No worries, okay?"

"Okay" she smiles weak eyes sad and thirsty...

Walking down Garry Street we cross Smith take a left sun gone down still afternoon my friend slowly coming into focus as I continue to talk about life death the universe she smiles lights a cigarette nods her head starts talking in pauses then laughing and moving to the rhythm of sun-go-down her personality spilling out into the streets, seen hundreds of fights like that last one I say, always a bummer, always quickly forgotten, the hell with the lot of you, we find ourselves on Smith Street corner of York jazz bar right there neon calling me I take her hand and run full speed into the bar man, honky tonk New Orleans jazz band on stage little white guy with shades doing miracles on the clarinet, fat guy with gray hair plays the hollow body guitar wiry grin, black guy on stand-up bass like fire spins it around baby be-bop hell man, we move toward the bar I slip and almost take down a tray of glasses continue moving, my friend grooving past me I see her motion "two" to the bartender then do the stirring thing with her finger, we sit and two martinis appear in front of us, she pays with a fifty,

"You should always shake a martini, not stir it" I say

She sticks her tongue out shakes her thing, band continues 8 or 10 people in the whole place mostly lonely people nothing to do, nowhere to go, not a bad scene, not much electric but not bad, music stupendous always loved jazz my friend's smiling at me pointing to the stage giving me the OK sign trumpet wailing "it's alright, man, it's alright" slow song now highlighted by piano solo electra glide down the street like it's that easy (and it is says the Buddha, go on, try it) she moves closer to me eyes on the stage I feel the warmth of her forearm on mine song builds to a crescendo then slows down again she crosses her legs foot hits mine, sorry she says smiles, alright I say, listen to the piano as the clarinet cuts in, then the rest of the horns, few moments in life like these, very very few, song in full swing steady rhythm we're almost drunk showing great poise and wild inclinations out of place and time except for the music, song ends, musicians stumble off the stage I turn to my friend and start talking,

"Strange life this is"

"Oh yeah, mmm"

"People are lonely"

"Yes, but what made you say that?"

"Look around..."

"...I see what you mean, but it's alright with me"

"So have you been to New Orleans?"

"Oh yeah"

"One of the few places of the world I want to see"

"From what I've seen of you, it's got your name written all over it"

"Juicy"

"I think Yonge Street in Toronto would suit you fine too"

"I think right here, right now, suits me fine...ever hear of Ken Finkleman?"

"Isn't he that Canadian filmmaker?"

"Yeah, ever seen his TV show 'The Newsroom'?"

"Haven't seen anything from him, why?"

"You should treat yourself...Canadian movies and television are among the best on the planet"

"I don't think I agree with you, they're not nearly as good as European movies, especially the Italian and the French"

"Please, spare me that Eurotrash, self-congratulatory, arthouse bullshit, a woman yearning for three hours doesn't do it for me"

She laughs and laughs and laughs,

"Okay, okay" she says "don't pull any punches now"

"Fellini, however, is the king of all things"

"I like Rossellini better, but, yeah, Fellini"

"How about De Sica or Bergman?"

"Yeah, oh yeah"

"Spiderman was a great movie"

"I hate that mainstream shit"

"Mainstream? That was a great movie about, oh fuck it, look, I challenge you to present a better filmmaker than Atom Egoyan"

"The hell with him"

"I'll have a Scotch and water, lots of ice"

She actually gets up and orders a couple, wry smile, hips bouncing, eyes like jewels, legs like whiskey, she walks down the bar past bartender in black tie lights a cigarette blows out smoke rising in blue streaks reminds me of things gone awry, gone like Modesty Blaise in junky whorehouse, psychedelic pleasure with pumpkin permanently erect in the dead water, bartender says something they're in conversation she glances at me between words he smiles that 'fuck me' smile uh-huh, she touches his arm says goodbye moving in my direction I begin to laugh hard and harder she turns serious sits down,

"Are you having a good fucking time?" she says,

"Wanna split?"

We begin to move towards the exit and back to the world down icy sidewalk I take a few steps, slide, a few steps, repeat, cars are everywhere man she says inhaling the exhaust while lighting a cig cruising down Donald Street resting on St. Mary's large hotel limousine in front of it doorman kissing ass we look for awhile blowing clouds of ice-cold air into the sky three foot snow-banks line the sidewalks streets busy with end-of-day shit car-horns lights and sirens everywhere dark sky seems sad somehow, fuck it I say, laugh loud crazy mad and distant,

"You've got a rough complexion" she says moving forward,

"Yeah, kinda shitty"

"Not at all, it's symbolic"

"Of my extended adolescence, I know, let's keep moving, got a smoke?"

Damn my scraggy face pack comes out red Du Mauriers looking beautiful one goes to my lips my friend pulls out her flask we're sharing whiskey old old Native man slowly passes us black beard dotted with gray lines etched deep into his face around the eyes thin jean jacket wrapped tight, Middle Eastern Man smokes brown cig outside department store smiles at us I shake his hand and move on, through the confused traffic two young boys slide down street invulnerable magic we're on Portage Avenue city's main artery Holiday lights on every lamppost red blue green orange purple reflecting off large glass building covers three blocks across the street there's a head-shop, then an old music store, a bar and a cigar store, drunks move through the working crowd hands out with the rest of the sadness and wonder and absolute bullshit I'm thinking about how much I like The Screaming Blue Messiahs and DOA and The Replacements and The Del Fuegos and The Wonderstuff and The Pixies and Lou Reed's "Rock and Roll Animal" and Joe Strummer And The Mescaleros' "Streetcore", a sharp harmonica solo comes into mind memories of hundreds of blues bands I've seen at The Windsor Hotel which is where I suggest we go next my friend smiling her approval starts talking confident rapid-like I listen to every word something about music the state of society sounds like anarchist punk-drunk thinking sprinkled with kindness almost hippie-like, that's it, she's half-punk half-hippie, a prototype you might say on and on with it snow falling a bit heavier leaving footprints in our half-hippie half-punk wake,

"My uncle saw Jimi Hendrix live in San Diego in 1967"

"At a small or large place?"

"Small, about 300 people"

"That's fucking great"

"You like Jimi?"

"Oh yeah"

"Juicy...by the way, I meant it was symbolic of how you live, you know, rough and tough, rock and roll survivor..."

Sweet sugar kisses on my cheek she smiles,

"Uh, okay, let's move out before I fuck ya on the street"

She punches my arm as I run across the ice and cement laughing her giggles behind me thinking 'bout a foot job I received under a table once at a downtown diner, then thinking 'bout the fact I've probably lost my job visions of eviction notices and dodging the landlord, too familiar with that shit man, we continue down the street wandering through the late afternoon mire reach Portage and Main wind howling round the buildings like a tornado cigarette blows out of my mouth snow blinding in our eyes, ears everything white as death on the corner my friend hangs on to me,

"LET'S GET INSIDE" I shout over the wind and snow,

We run to a skyscraper open the doors huddle in lobby suits and ties and skirts everywhere we start laughing at the sheer insanity and improbability of it all,

"Always loved that street corner" she laughs,

"It's a trip"

There are walkways and underground tunnels connecting building to building all over downtown that's where we are in the underground busker leans on wall singing Nirvana songs my friend throws a loony in guitar case we sit on the steps and listen to the music this fucker even has the Cobain growl guitar chords a bit off but that's okay cuz it's only rock and roll, I notice my friend staring at me acting like I don't know what's going on things getting tight and easy this young broad really works for me we're in an easy groove arguing and laughing disagree on many things and even that feels right at this particular moment in this particular place hunkering up to a streeeeet musician laying the tunes feels right (death just round the corner) feels good and alive (death round the corner) my friend starts talking,

"I gave a guy a hand job under the table at a bar once"

"No shit"

"The waitress would come around as I stroked him and ordered drinks like nothing doing here baby...it was great"

"Did he have a big cock?"

Busker starts with the hippie crap, Joni Mitchell, CSNY, all that,

"This guy's starting to get on my nerves" I say,

"Just a few more songs, here"

I take the flask hiding it from the crowd small sips burning all the way down my throat guts on fire explosion of mind I shut my eyes let the booze and pot work me in certain directions, colors come first as an idea, then literally electric orange streetlights catapults in the distance causing eruptions of green takes shape human figure slightly visible then deadly rainbow crumbling to the mud and guts like the rest of us, all cheering for the next round mouth open breath comes out in clouds hippie shit in background breaks it up, goddamn it, I snap out of it and gather myself c'mon man, don't want to look like a pretentious prick, do you?

Slow-mo-girl sitting across from busker staring straight ahead I look closer who is this rock and roll chick? Of all the lonely sounds out there, how did she happen to invade mine? Busker takes a break we start talking about his guitar tell him I used to play in a band had a Les Paul and a B.C. Rich, used to call it the rich bitch cuz it sounded wild like a buzzsaw, guy says he prefers the Fender sound to the Gibson or Rich, sure if you play that hippie shit I say, he's taken aback by this and withdraws I wave my friend over we begin moving on down the aisle past all the people in this massive hurry to get somewhere and do something, everyone head down trying to forget the bullshit, trying to forget we made the world and we're going to destroy it, but

my friend has large smile and oval green eyes laughing
all the time but tough as nails street-girl intellectual a
particular energy I've felt rarely in my life love her
large curly black hair so thick it almost reaches the edge
of her shoulders moves like an afro but not quite we
reach a record store Goth girl behind counter I got my
eye on her she's tall and mean-looking good stuff I'm
thinking, good stuff, my friend flipping through CD's
picks out something from The Velvet Underground
getting along with Goth girl sticks her tongue out as
they laugh I feel completely excluded they continue
talking about various bands and this bar and that bar
I'm getting tired of the whole thing but being polite cuz
you gotta in this gin-soaked reality and cuz Goth girl's
pierced tongue keeps sliding forward she's got sex on
her mind I make mental note to return to this store by
myself my friend buys the CD we the get fuck out of
here...

Girl-friend has a Samosa we sit at a table watch
people walk by making assumptions on who they are see
balding man somewhere in his late forties I say he has a

conservative car, two kids and a wife who hates him, my
friend points to a woman with hair pinned-up tight
office mini-skirt red pumps says she's a nymphomaniac,
I like to think she's right about that one, so we continue
like this the sadness separating everyone from
themselves, the beauty as well, all too confusing for any
one of us to decipher we've got the ideas and the
theories and the sonnets and the literature, art, high
paying jobs, beautiful lovers, gigantic telescopes,
astronomy, religion, philosophy, nice convertible
cruising down the avenue joe-six-pack waving at the
chicks Elvis Presley hair blowing in the wind sideburns
down to his jawbone four-wheel steel-machine like a
shark slicing through schools of infant water babies
convinced he's doing right living well lights cigarette
takes a puff flicks it to the street hits old lady on head
she's feeling righteous man, nothing but ideas, guy in
his thirties slicked-back hair three hundred dollar suit
pauses in the middle of the food-court and looks around
like it's all his creation he sees us ignores me focuses on
my friend he smiles she winks and gives him the finger,
he moves towards us I wave him away he complies my
scruffy beard and long hair working in the right

direction, little does he know I'm almost a pacifist, about 85% of me, slickster might even have kicked my ass but fuck him...my friend leaning back with finger to her temple looking pensive turtleneck highlighting her face she looks tough at a glance sensitive eyes almost cruel mouth when she's not smiling big lips long chunky thighs black eye-liner deep red lipstick I could eat her alive given a chance our eyes meet then clumsily turn away "time for a drink" I say, we start running...

Towards the exit out the door cross the street Portage and Main behind us so is the wind feels warm out here snow falling slowly in thick flakes passing shitty bars on each corner someone arguing at every entrance ain't no damn good but we continue cuz no place better than this one looking ahead and elsewhere a vile cowardly act all together impossible to attain nothing out there but yourself and the immediacy of the moment as I take my friend's hand she smiles blows out smoke old Chevy sits at curb I get a lung-full of car exhaust, banning smoking in bars, ridiculous...she starts talking about her family serious expression boyfriend back in Toronto things real shitty there,

"I've gotta break this fucking thing off!"

"What are you waiting for, just do it, he's just another fucking guy"

"I know, I know, we're already broken up, nobody's verbalized it yet, that's all"

"Well, nothing's as easy as it should be"

"There you go being the guru again"

"Kid Dynomite baby"

"Funneeeeeee guy"

"Listen, I've got a story"

"Alright, alright"

"When I was seventeen I ended up fucking two best friends for a week straight on alternate nights with out them finding out"

"But eventually?"

"They found out"

"And therein lies the moral of the story"

"Slow down kitty-kat"

"So who's your favorite Canadian writer?"

"That's easy, Michael Turner, hands down"

"Hard Core Logo, right?"

"Right"

"Evelyn Lau can really write man"

"Bet your ass she can, better than all that shit that's considered so great"

"What do you mean?"

"You know, the so-called great Canadian writers, the Canadian royalty as it is, Margaret Atwood, Timothy Findlay, Alice Munro, Robertson Davies, Margaret Lawrence, they call that writing? What the hell is that crap?"

"No argument here, don't like any of that stuff, have a particular dislike for Atwood"

"Mordecai Richler is the only saving grace among the well known Canadian writers...most of my favorite writers are American anyway"

"Why do you think that is?"

"Don't know, just turned out that way, why, are you a racist?"

"Funny, I never saw anti-american as being racist"

"Well isn't it?"

"I suppose it is...but I'm not anti-american, I just hate their foreign policy, anyway all I meant was that maybe there was something in American culture that helped shape the type of writer you like"

"Unlikely, I don't care where the fucking writer comes from, ya dig?"

"Dig, but you underestimate the effect culture and surrounding have on someone's fucking art (she takes a puff and blows out smoke) and I should slap you silly for that look in your eye"

"Check it out"

Drunken Native fellow sits on curb in front of the old Metropolitan Theatre holds cup out black eye missing teeth I flip him a loony knowing damn well nothing is solved keep moving eyes forward this corner grim silent construction site on the left a skeleton building sits waiting looks like bombed out pictures from world war two craters bricks piled high bulldozers two hundred foot cranes top covered in snow library closed down for renovations boarded up thrift shops and record stores seems everything coming to a halt before final plunge yet impossible to let go of nothing to do but keep moving stark beauty in seeing for the first time a smile and a wink nothing doing hot day on the grass at Assiniboine Park sparking reefer women in daisy-dukes listening to loud music outside parked Camaro with scoop on hood someone kicks a soccer ball lights a smoke I'm kissing another human she's young and beautiful and entirely with me wrestle on the grass like a blues riff in E deep deep blue sky sun rays killing us slowly in the middle of laughing loving and working we will not be interrupted...

"There are parts of this city...pretty dismal" she says

"I hear ya"

"It feels like it's unfinished somehow"

"It's a place in transition, so where are you staying?"

"In The Osborne Village, where else?"

"By yourself or...?"

"By myself, but that's a long story"

"Got no time for long stories, sister"

I cross the street without waiting start moving up the sidewalk she follows my direction from other side quick pace lights cigarette passes a few people I see her eyes looking for me through the crowd even though she pretends she's not pause in traffic she bolts across starts talking immediately about this book she read 'The Doors of Perception' by Huxley, good read I tell her, got a light? Got lighter to my face I hand it back to her, now she's talking about Kurt Vonnegut real fast and almost nervous-like waving her hands hair bouncing from side to side, uh-huh I say, alright curly-moe give me a chance, she continues I listen with pleasure cuz it's okay, and it's alright, blowing smoke at the stars above sirens and car-horns surround us, music comes from an open door of a pub, laughter and bottles clanking someone telling someone to fuck off, couple of teenagers fly down the sidewalk singing "I Wanna Be Sedated", crescent moon hanging above steam rises from every building looks like city's on fire in the −20 night coming fast streets thinning out suburbanites got their dinners on the table and their annoying fat-assed kids begging for more downtown crowd starts to come out some already drunk from the morning session going home to crash, others just waking up looking for the vibe or someone to fuck over, it's hangover Thursday in a drinking city outcome foretold possibilities unlikely, electricity slicing down the back alleys in waves of shot-glass fever, we're hanging out in front of a church talking to an old Filipino lady used to work in the dishpit with me, she's telling me I look ragged and beat as always, but I forgot, she says, you're mister cool ain't ya, my friend already inside her head they're talking intently, smiling and talking smooth motion I make them both laugh we say good bye as her bus pulls up, take a sip off the flask save last one for her we're moving on up baby, make our way down the frozen sidewalk towards the Windsor Hotel pass old church spirals reaching upwards failing miserably, us we're moving along while the black and gray settle in, broken bottle spills dark liquor on snow looks like blood in the street-light orange, ambulance slices in and out of traffic red lights reflecting off glass building, what a fantastic jip, what a complete wack-job, we're watching it under the prairie moon like raw eggs in the grim-city sunlight ain't nothing like your backyard man silent wisp out your ass full motion poetry while digging for gold in a sewer sewage gone mad my friend smiles at me I find a back alley she pulls out a joint I kiss her quickly playfully she sparks the joint in crosstown traffic light says red but we continue...

Large mural of vaudeville acts on the side of The Windsor Hotel including Charlie Chaplain who once stayed here in the early nineteen hundreds, wrote a letter to his brother from room 23 saying he was going to quit vaudeville and get into the pictures as they called them, we're standing outside admiring the mural thinking about Charlie Chaplain cigarette in mouth I suddenly get strong thirst for alcohol take my friend by the arm and move through the steel door telling her in summer there are fender to fender Harleys out front, large rectangle room the odd pillar stage at the front pool tables at the back VLT's line the walls I reach the bar order a Heineken (seems to be my friend's favorite) and a scotch and water for me, we take a table on the side there are red terri-cloth covers on every one of them,

"Never seen this before" says my friend touching the terri-cloth,

"What's this playing, is that Muddy waters?"

"Thanks for the drink, I got something to tell you"

"Shoot"

"We used to bush-party a lot in Pukatawagon and I remember getting fucked on top of a rock not to far from the party, my back was arched over it and my boyfriend kept sliding in and out of me, slipping off, the back of my head hitting the rock, hurt like hell, it was great"

"Was this the same guy with the hand-job under the table?"

"No, no, they're years apart, I was seventeen on the rock"

"Yes, I see"

"Hurt like hell"

'What was your boyfriend like?"

"He was a Rez kid, you know...played bass in a band...they were pretty shitty if I remember...the first time we moved to a big city my old man got stationed in San Francisco, so you can imagine...I went and got myself a mohawk the first week, green on one side (she waves a hand) red on the other (waves hand on other side)"

"So your old man was in the American military?"

"No, he was in the Canadian Intelligence business, top secret"

"You're a crazy punk, make no mistake about it"

Old lady in corner with blue wig all twisted perched on top smeared lipstick ragged nightgown we call her the witch, sits and talks to herself while downing draft try to approach her and she hisses like a viper, saw her in back alley once pissing by garbage bin hissing at me while squatting in the filth and broken beer bottles, owner of the place very large Greek man tending bar no nonsense tough guy from the old country when bar is dead he plays VLT's at the back stroking his mustache drinking scotch on the rocks, couple of drunk guys at a table argue about nothing, one Native, one white, both stupid, black guy sits at bar smoking cigarillos, middle-aged couple by the stage look more suited for the opera drinking beer out of large mugs red-faced and happy, tapping my temple I'm thinking hmmmm, hmmmm,

"I remember having sex at Vimmy Ridge Park during the day once" I say "there were lots of people around, kids throwing frisbees, couples holding hands like they're hot-shit, you know what I mean, we were by a small bush pretending we were having a romantic moment in the sun but we were actually fucking under the blanket...whenever someone got close we just kind of stopped with these shit grins on our faces, "hello", "nice day", when they moved on we would slowly start up again keeping one eye on the park and one on each other...did the same thing in a car with the same woman, jogger kept running back and forth right by us pretending not to know what was going on..."

"You're a dog"

"A hound, to be sure"

"What's with that old lady?"

"They call her the witch, been here forever, lives upstairs in the hotel, very old, very drunk, very senile"

"Kind of sad"

'I don't think so"

"What's happy about it?"

"It's not happy either, it just IS...how are you going to be at the end?"

"I don't know"

"Exactly, none of us know, that old lady's probably had some really good times in her life...now her gas tank's empty, she's running on fumes...what the hell, you can't laugh all the time"

"So pain in life is payment for the good times, is that what you mean?"

"More about balance than payment, a way of reminding yourself nothing lasts, and that's not a sad thing, on the contrary, if everyone truly took that to heart they'd be happier"

"How do you mean?"

"Imagine how much you would enjoy a moment if you really believed in impermanence, I mean really believed it?"

"I don't think that's possible"

Tune changes to Sunhouse that finger-picking delta blues does it like no other animal crouching in the corner we're a bit confused our minds in overdrive so I focus on the music and let it take me elsewhere brain healthy in tune with reality nothing wrong with drifting sometimes as far away as possible my friend starts talking again about my impermanence theory, I listen but not really, that guitar riff has me I tell you, there are pictures and paintings of blues legends all over the walls, biggest one being B. B. King playing Lucille under a cloudy sky, I notice musicians carrying their instruments to the stage, drum kit being assembled, some talking going on about lights sound whatever else, all familiar faces from the local blues scene I realize there's a jam going on, open stage, done the jam thing many times in the past but suddenly very happy I'm no longer part of that scene, no desire whatsoever to perform, strange when you consider it used to be my greatest passion, very very strange my friend sitting back cool as ice sipping on her Heineken like a pro, bouncer walks in tall thin guy handlebar mustache been doing this rock and roll baby for an eternity hangs with the bikers tough guy never smiles he's talking to the musicians now, points to the left side of the stage angry shouting, "y'see, I guarantee it!" Walks back to his post like he's the fucking king crimson, lights a smoke, cracks a beer and sits back...

First group of musicians up there start doing a jig, more country than blues but still alright, singer has flood pants and white socks baseball cap plays a Fender Tele sings a bit like Stomping Tom Connors, his rhythm straight up E after A after C and so on, my friend's bopping her head, tough guys by pool table lean forwards, I'm smoking cigarettes like they're going out of style (which they are) drinking Scotch and water out of a thin short glass, bass player young black guy plays the root note not much else groovin' in time still time well wasted, lead man slings a wicked axe hollow-body Gibson easing the licks into the room they're doing Albert Collins now, then they're done, leave the stage to a lukewarm response cuz nobody gives a shit about nothing, guy hosting the gig says "we'll be right back with new musicians after a short break, if you wanna sign up for a jam talk to Louie over there", well well, tap on my shoulder guy I know guitar in hand starts talking non-stop immediately about his music, his art, his life, okay okay I motion him to a chair and point him in the other direction he starts talking to slow-motion-girl she's right in there man, I walk to the can feeling slow and easy and smooth as silk and leather door opens smell of piss right up my nostrils I take a position, guy stumbles out of stall and right out the door, I do my thing hear the jam start up again, walk past pool table big motherfucker leather vest stick in hand he's looking at the balls thinking, "hmmm, uh-huh, hmmm", reach my table bus-stop-girl there alone,

"Where's that guitar player guy?"

"I told him to fuck-off" she says

"No really, where is he?"

"I'm sorry if he's your friend, but he was driving me up the fucking wall"

"It's alright, he's not my friend, he just thinks he is..." I point to the stage "How are these clowns?"

She waves a hand like it all means nothing and she's happy about it yet there's something behind those wolf-eyes pushing at the edge snarling silverback raging through the alleyways it's my ass on the line, frail sickly fellow on stage plays the harmonica like it's a gift from Satan himself, it wails through the entire room in large splashes of red and black, even the assholes at the back tilt their heads and wonder, I wish for only one goddamn thing, that this harmonica riff never stops...and then it does...

We're both up at the bar talking with the bartender my friend gets tap on shoulder from buxom brunette they hug and kiss obviously very happy about something my friend introduces us they know each other from up north somehow good feeling to be in the middle of two beautiful Native chicks her friend seems very easy and relaxed no problem talking with her likes her grass and booze rock and roll even the occasional novel turns her crank I'm pretty much listening to old drunk friends catch up both leaning forward new arrival long straight jet-black hair thicker than the devil's I sit and smile take a drink have a smoke the witch looking at me smiling she holds up a piece of paper I walk over it's a drawing of a red rose in crayons, "five bucks" she says I give it to her, she shows me two more, one a lilac one a white rose, I wave my hand walk away show my friends this rose in no time the other two drawings are on the terri-cloth they seem to think they've bought a piece of The Windsor for five bucks a pop I look at the witch, a wave of sadness runs down my spine...

There's a familiar shape at the top of the stairs leading to the hotel, old friend of mine named Frank, haven't seen him in years, I tap my friend on the shoulder and point in the direction, she looks, no one's there,

"Listen" I say "I thought I saw an old friend of mine upstairs, I'm going to talk with him for a bit, wait for me"

They nod barely hearing what I say I move up the stairs past the coffee-shop and the beer vendor see Frank's back ahead of me and call out to him, he doesn't hear door closes behind him I follow, once again he's slightly ahead of me going up the stairs I see his pant leg on the next level, I see it stop, he notices me and there's that big fucking smile from ear to ear, we hug and do the street thing he's looking good long black ponytail streaks of gray down to his ass dark Native complexion I follow him to his room, up the stairs and through hallways with green wallpaper that doesn't stick properly, young guy with leather jacket hangover-pale-face passes us Frank gives him a nod, we reach his door number twenty three and we're inside empty beer bottles everywhere smells like booze and stale cigarettes, I sit down and take a long look,

"So how's it going, Frank?"

"It's good my man, couldn't be better...just sold two paintings for 300 each, got some blow, want to do a line?"

"No, but go ahead"

He starts cutting the lines and snorting them down followed by large gulps of beer,

"Still paying alimony for my five kids back East, you know...lotsa scratch..."

"Got a job on the side, or is it all your art?"

"It's all the art man, it will never be anything but...y'see, a real artist would rather starve than do something he doesn't like...I told myself years ago the only way I'm going to earn money is through my art, no bullshit job, no welfare, nothing else man"

"Good to hear"

More lines...

"Man, remember those three young chicks we picked up at the old Blue Note?"

"Didn't know they were underage, man"

"Like that would have stopped you, c'mon, we're smarter than that...everybody knows you're a class act, you just act like you're not"

"You give me too much credit, Frank"

He puts his head down suddenly sad no need for words I see hear and feel clearly, he looks back up feint smile,

"Did you ever read that kick-ass review I got for my show in Toronto?"

"I believe I did...every word true, of course"

"Y'know, in all these years I've hardly ever gotten a bad review, only once or twice"

"They don't mean shit anyway"

"How's your writing, man?"

"Not much recognition, very little money, besides that, couldn't be better"

"I read your novel at the library last month...best thing in that dump"

"Won't argue with you, thingamajig...are you still going out with that young chick from The Blue Note?"

"No, broke up last week...man, this time it really stings"

"I seem to recall telling you not to lose your head over this one"

"Yeah, she was only seventeen...met her parents, we actually got along well, can you imagine? White parents liking their seventeen year old daughter's thirty-seven year old crazy-ass Indian boyfriend?"

"Hard to imagine, I know"

"An artist to boot, no future, no money, all that shit, man...they were pretty damn cool, real left-wing liberals, you know..."

We sit around drinking beer and talking about everything we can wrap our heads around laughing smoking sunlight coming through the shades in thin beams he's a good man sparks a joint turns the radio on to Joe Jackson followed by REM and The Jesus And

Mary Chain there's a cockroach in the corner it makes me laugh thinking about this day think briefly about my job then say fuck it shake Frank's hand and do the twist early evening joyfully participating in the world's troubles I keep telling him not to worry about his girl ain't no worry man there are many bullshit wonders in this life he's doing more lines talking faster by the minute fast talking guru in jean jacket scruffy goatee we're shaking hands under the dim light outside world nothing but a bother pain in the ass reality ain't nothing to us locked away in tiny room inside Windsor Hotel music coming from the floor boards guitar riffs and bass solos he's looking at me like he wants to say something radio playing an old Kiss song he hands me a beer devil in our corner, BANG outside the door older fellow in brown leather jacket comes in blue baseball cap gray hair gray stubble he's an old drunk lives down the hall whistling some serious hell joins us in our sit-down cracks a beer followed by a mighty gulp he's doing the classic drunken slur sounds like caricature only this time it's real I listen to him and to Frank and consider myself the lesser of three people, two other guys come in, one an ex-con, the other a small time pot dealer, we're all shaking hands and lifting our beer to our mouths, ex-con takes off jacket large biceps starts flexing "touch this" he says, I pretend I'm impressed by all this horse-shit, uh-huh, yeah, I forgive you, things are moving quite fast makes me think about Blake for a brief instant what he said about excess and heavenly glory, ex-con starts pounding old guy in the ribs, old guy laughing but in pain stands there and takes it, then pot dealer takes a jab, old guy "ha ha ha ugggh shit", they sit down we have more beer and cigarettes Frank holding court talking about ballin' some chick he met downstairs at the bar we're all laughing and howling, ex-con pounds old man in ribs a few times then sits down, has a gulp of beer starts talking to me about jail and all the good boys in there, seems jail is full of nothing but stand-up guys according to this fucker, pot dealer complaining about lack of money, Frank staring into space one by one they start leaving like in a trance out the door then it's just me and Frank...sad smile on his face he begins to fade, I see the rope burns on his neck, room covered in empty beer bottles, few lines of coke on the table, he fades a bit more, then he's gone...I pause for a moment to look around, alone I get up, let myself out the door quietly close it behind me walk down the hall with red wallpaper coming unglued reach the stairwell hear the blues coming from the bar young East Indian fellow drunkenly comes up the stairs goes right by me without a glance, there's a landing between first floor and basement windows facing North I sit and light a cigarette look out the window into the night down the frozen street finish smoke move towards the hall, hear footsteps see my bus-stop friend wandering the hallway putting her ear to the doors I call out to her, hey she says quirky smile picks up pace,

"My friend left so I thought I'd see if I could find you"

"Right on..what's going on down there?"

"Some good musicians, some mediocre ones...how about you, find your friend?"

"Yeah...he's gone"

I take her arm and lead her down to the bar, hey look at that she says...

Back door of the bar we're smoking a joint with some patrons tough pool players seem alright, back alley littered in garbage feels warm out here dead of winter we're without jackets shooting the shit, finish joint get inside blues band playing Hendrix "All Along The Watchtower", damn boring sight I grab my jacket point to the door "my thoughts exactly" says my friend's expression, straight out into the winter somewhere around the –20 mark feels great cuz we're drunk and stoned and like all other human beings are partially endowed with free will, enough to lose jobs and meet strangers at bus-stops, and fight for the right and bullshit till the day is done, and you can all come kiss my ass says the song lean up against a post watch the cars go by strike a match blow out smoke and the hell with it...

Cool easy riding up the boulevard she's talking to me like we're somehow connected by eons of bar crawling lingo type suicide jazz music eases you on your way I take her hand almost in slow motion I say almost cuz slow-mo-action don't do it for me slow rolling acoustic guitar neon lights and slow burning fires somewhere in groove with your sick and twisted simulations street-core punk rocker hip-hop bullshit far as I'm concerned it's easy days leisure electric buzz cruise the edge if needed mental gymnastics no problem all too familiar song picks up now saxophone moving double time bass player sounds too crazy brain on fire Chet Baker's dead all that makes sense gone with him and you on your treadmill disaster feed a hungry kid you fucking prick listen to that bass jumbo jumbo Dean Martin slickster too cool and relaxed (nobody that easy fool!) ain't no angel man ain't no devil playing tug-a-war with my personality folk singer wasting precious street corners on nothing at all hate no one with sense of ease and kindness she smilin' in the ice-cold hostile reality all too fragile all too busted seems secret very simple just don't fuck your neighbor around somehow impossible for us to follow too complicated for primates working it out in the trees with our wooden clubs and bent-backwards psyches my secret love affair and private confession one day I will tell you everything tattered from life abundant in grace and smoooooth luck cuz it ain't impossible says the idiot and the brothers Karamazov there's a suitcase on the street leather tassels with hobo buried in snow junky syringe not too far welfare mother smokes in the sunlight 10 year old kid runs down the piazza, my friend takes my hand willingly and looks at me...."Hello" she says unzips her jacket cigarette dangling from her red red lips wiry grin, sky black as it gets lights buzzing from buildings green blue red everything tempered with streetlight-orange man, we walk in silence for awhile feeling good in the downtown quiet-sad, we stop for cigarettes at a hotel I notice a few tears in my friend's eyes as she pays, you alright I say? Outside she hugs me and I return the favor hear the crying her body shaking "it's no good" she says "it's no good", "hey let's cross the street" I say "things look different over there" alright she gathers herself and follows, we hang around on the corner of Donald and Ellice smoke our ten thousandth cigarette, our bodies in some kind of forgotten rhythm, our minds in that strange place, walking towards The Exchange District in downtown Winnipeg on Ellice Avenue probably means nothing to the left fucking bank of Paris so let's get funky on equal terms,

"Sorry about that..." she says,

"No problem at all...you okay?"

"Sure"

"Oh shit"

"What?"

Guy I know tall and lanky mid-fifties downtown scruff small time criminal bullshit extraordinaire coming towards us I think of running right there and then but he sees us stupid grin on his face says "aren't I cool and dangerous?", shakes my hand, shakes my friend's hand thin red hair, red beard awful teeth worse than mine this guy a real pain in the ass actually believes his own bullshit this guy's sick I tell you, wrote a few good plays that were put on at The West End Cultural Center fucker used to sit in the back and laugh out loud to all the jokes,

"Working on another play right now, gonna be great, I like her" he says pointing to my friend homemade cigarette between dirty fingernails "you should see the broad I'm balling"

I'm polite but rather cold hoping this moron can sense it sending out all sorts of bad vibes my friend feels it immediately almost in shock at my simmering anger, but this idiot, this idiot continues like it's a sunny day in the Caribbean and we got all the time in the world,

"You guys don't know fuck-all, far too young, I slept with Kathleen Turner once, she was here doing one of my plays, crazy fucking broad..."

Every word like a scalpel slicing through my brain he laughs after everything he says,

"Broke a guy's jaw in twenty three places once during a martial arts tournament, didn't win the damn thing but I fucked the owner of the Main Street school, she's a third degree black belt, said there was still some shit I could teach her"

He continues, continues, killing every moment with impunity I ready my self for a strike my friend explodes,

"Get the fuck away from us right fucking now!" she screams,

"What the fuck..." he says

"Right now! I don't want to hear any fucking stories, not a goddamn word, nothing you fucking...ugggh, do you realize how much precious time you're killing? Do you know what delusional means, you ugly prick? Listen, we are going to take a left right here and you are not, dig?"

He looks at me in a state of shock,

"Yeah" I say "what she said"

We take the left and, just like that, he's gone beautiful day in the neighborhood I cheer my friend look behind see his shadow hunched over watching us as we move away slight tinge of pity comes over me I decide then and there to apologize to him next time, chick was crazy man you know? Lot worse people than this poor bastard in the world but the hell with him, keep moving through this overgrown small town people on the streets everyone wasted looking for a good time I feel alive out here, do the spin-doctor-hurdle, fuzzy guitar mescaline illusion time to ride the wave to its logical conclusion, Robin Trower played a mean guitar back in the seventies check out his live record look for the dream-guitar to take you somewhere else spark a joint and say ooohah, slow-mo-girl cruising the sidewalk beside me feels damn fine and on fire, living how one chooses most precious thing in the world, Dead Kennedys kicked some real ass young and full of angst-ridden shit real-time baby, old Native guy hooked on hairspray asks for money I give him some he kisses my hand and says "god bless you" been seeing this guy for at least ten years hanging out on Portage and Main down Hargrave and

Cunberland round Central Park and Q'uappelle street, I feel embarrassed cuz he's fought a much longer and tougher battle than I have, we keep moving my friend talking about her boyfriend once again I listen I feel she needs it she's talking cool and easy about her travels a hint of pain in her voice says she would hang her hat in Winnipeg if given the right reason keep moving I say,

"Thought you didn't like to travel" she says,

"I don't, but you do, you need it"

"The Master has spoken"

"Got a smoke? I need a beer...gotta be careful, I'm running out of money"

"Money, for today, is absolutely meaningless"

"Is that right?"

"Can you promise me that? Let's do a blood oath on it, today money is absolutely meaningless"

"As long as you're paying, you got it"

"Cocksucker"

Sidewalk going by in a blur screaming "if you want blood, you got it" there was a time when I felt at ease around people was natural leader young and tough now swing back and forth between wild-drunk-happy and pot-smoking recluse impulsive as ever feel rebellious

and downright nasty content with few possessions still
got the grim light needed for art, bus-stop girl singing
"Sex Gorilla" from National Velvet as she balances on
curb I see sadness creeping through it's the way of the
Tao nature will prevail so I'm told don't put much
stock in anything man-made including philosophies
ancient or new believe nothing nobody a gust of wind
leads us in another direction I take my friend into The
Ox downtown hotel bar on main floor strippers every
hour red carpet dirty glasses small round tables
scattered across the room woman at door has the shakes
head moves from side to side, usual crowd couple of
suits most core area derelicts odd jobs janitors
dishwashers welfare bums hotel denizens from upstairs
small time criminals uncombed hair looking for a buck
smoking home-made rollies, we take a small table at the
side of the stage fireman's pole in the middle of course
cliches come alive in these places see my neighbor sixty
seven years old got Players Light jammed into her
mouth suffered first heart attack last year guzzling
draft at far table old fucker with her bald head long
beard drinks hard stuff cigarillo in hand, waitress
young woman in her twenties recognizes me barely

smiles I make the motion she understands two drafts in front of us, my friend pays and smiles then frowns lights a cigarette blows out huge cloud of blue smoke goes into the ceiling and the rafters round the stage-lights blends with larger cloud canopy of blue-green smoke over our heads, guy in suit laughs with other guy in suit, drunk in the corner wild-eyed and desperate, first stripper comes to the stage tall blond muscular thighs, my friend starts smiling passes me lit smoke, stripper in one piece satin high-cut showing lots of leg and cheek, she moves slowly to an Aerosmith ballad up and around the pole tits popping out like ripe melons harvest time in the orgy hills, crowd into it howling at the machine, glasses raised in small victory, girl touches her cunt strokes the lips bar goes crazy, my friend gives the wolf call I down some draft bang my head here goes another, waving her ass in the air all around the room she's got us I tell you, she's got us...

Long blonde curls swing our way we've got a profile view stripper barely notices us my friend shifts her focus from her to me, her to me, I pretend I'm not aware of this and continue in my own fashion I have fought long and hard to maintain, man I'm rollercoaster Jim on electricity punk-drunk exuberant sexual deviant professional do-nothing loved by hundreds unaware of my deficiencies, AC/DC now on as blond beauty queen continues pumping her tits in our faces a solid fuck you to the middle class she's got round tits nipples not too large somewhat brown in color, down to her thongs she thrusts her pussy forward and retreats the whole time playing with her self in rhythm man, third and final song another rock ballad I'm already bored looking around the room for the next spark of fire, VLT's are full as always gambling never absent in the poorhouse guy stumbles into the washroom smell of urine comes into the bar stripper finished puts her clothes on at the side of the stage like it was her bedroom unaware of anyone else, always considered this the strangest part about the strip-bar experience, I urge my friend to finish her draft she downs it in one gulp follows me outside across the street into another hotel The Charley stripper just coming on rectangle room split in half by a long twisting u-shaped bar solid oak a thing of beauty to rest your elbows on, bartender short Chinese guy hair parted on side glasses white shirt black pants he's telling a drunk to fuck off in a thick accent, crowd same as across the street room more interesting small chandeliers wooden door frames two pool tables at the back large juke against the wall best music selection in town we sit at the bar six-foot brunette on stage a bit drunk thighs long and big ass sticks out like soccer ball very sexy I'm thinking, very dark pubic hair forms a triangle hair on head streaked with bright red lips like Snow White, calves like Mount Vesuvios, toes painted dark blue tattoo of dragon on left ass-cheek I see a friend across the bar long hair reporter red beard works for The Grain Commission approaches me we do the hippie shake introduce him to my friend, he sits with us we drink and smoke the minutes away talking the good talk this guy very interesting drunken intelligence all three of us getting along like we should, argument in far corner don't give a shit if bullets raze the bar down, to live in the moment doing nothing and everything is my absolute deepest heart's desire, losing my fucking job today best thing that could have happened cuz I saw the magic and I grabbed on, alcohol inside of me I feel it in my blood and everywhere else, legs holding strong as always, marijuana hovering round my brain as lucid as could be, reporter talking about the bullshit writing he has to do to pay the bills, writing about the state of our farm lands and related things,

"Well, farmers are important" I say,

"Nobody's disputing that...would you like to write about this shit?"

"That's a different story"

"I like what you're doing, I read your novel at the library, great stuff man, really liked it"

"God forbid that someone would actually buy a copy of the damn thing"

"What's that, I couldn't hear you, music's too loud"

"Led Zeppelin sucks, don't you think?"

"Oh yeah, Jurassic man, the most over-rated band in history...listen to 'Bikini Red' from The Screaming Blue Messiahs"

"Way ahead of you"

"Stripper's done, the other one should be just starting across the street, right?" says bus-stop girl,

"Fuck me please" says reporter "Please!"

We're all okay with it moving across the street half the bar behind us bartender left alone with his bullshit thoughts I open a door as stripper hits the stage short Filipino woman in unbelievable shape hard-body suicide this lady lean and mean, straight black hair down her back tickles her ass hips wide and strong light brown skin belly-button pierced mad eyes brown and green, tables now full drinks are ordered we sit closer to the stage but not in sniffer's row reporter friend talking to slow-mo-girl feeling like reggae queen in urban madness laughter coming out of me like Crown Royal at the corner brothel, everyone has lit cigarette in hand killing ourselves slowly just how we like it, don't give me no shit man ain't buying it stripper gyrating to ZZ top something from "Fandango" looking at crowd with sexy disdain ass jiggling despite the muscles few women in room seem distant bored and separate, in the washroom joints are lit and lines are snorted crack pipe is out everywhere I go lately eyes are vacant, lots of hard drugs to be found in any city I abstain always feeling the booze and grass enough for me and my way, see my friend she's staring at me through the haze and distance, see her say something to reporter they trade seats she's beside me punches my arm smiling eyes slightly watery we're talking again in the middle of naked bodies smoke-filled rooms desires running rampant the fringes of society all here for your viewing my reporter friend doing the same thing a bit shy and confused but eager nonetheless unafraid moving forward not backward this is something to remember a drink is spilled on my pant leg I laugh and don't give a fuck light a smoke forget about it lousy penny-pincher my old humpbacked hag of a caretaker still alive and drinking in love with something or someone no heroes to be had old age a distant reality not worth betting on bus-stop-girl's eyes are large oval like a wolf's intelligent and kind capable of cruelty like every last one of you motherfuckers...stripper now butt naked I'm ready to burst insanity and confusion all over myself she's slithering on a blanket sliding wet and groovy some ridiculous hip-hop song in the background reporter friend beside me got quite the paunch a very kind fellow making eye contact with stripper she's giving it back some dare and challenge in the room he's pointing to his crotch crowd is cheering she's making gestures playing with her tits playing the crowd and him with his tongue out he touches my shoulder in friendship stripper's done I feel a cool slide of jazzz motion as slow-mo-girl gets up plugs the juke and hits the dance floor...it's a jazzy song I can't figure out emphasis on that dreamy slow-ass bluesy guitar-run dance floor is to the right of stage she's alone on it jeans moving round her legs just right a few young Native women join her tight T-shirts tight jeans thick black heels all looking cute and okay in the orange rain reality they talk and dance and smoke and laugh and look down and look up and look sad and happy, reporter joins in moving awkward but not knowing it, whole scene very real and self-sufficient, women seem interested in reporter friend yet he hasn't had sex in two years, maybe too kind, maybe the gods are cruel, he's a gentler version of myself I'm thinking I'm more of a scoundrel I get laid every couple of months, while we're on the subject bus-stop friend moving like end of the world is around the corner, she's swaying gently from side to side sex is all around me, she's doing the alternative-rock-hurly-burly looking clumsy-sexual, feet almost stationary one in front of other knees bent hair crazy moving from side to side, yes, the gods are truly horrible and cruel, impressed by her ability to shimmy and slide after a day like this I give her the thumbs up like the jerk I am, she turns and glides to the table burning cigarette in ashtray, she inhales and blows out, cloud follows her back to dance floor reporter smiles at me takes a clumsy step everything looking hazy like a desert slow-motion-girl in easy groove song ends entire bar moves across the street for the next stripper, and it continues like that back and forth both bars staggering their strippers in agreement, a parade of the shiftless bankrupt and fringe-living cross the street every half hour or so some of us drinks in hand, young Native women with us howl at the oncoming traffic, naked flesh seems to be everywhere for the taking but all illusion, all impermanent just right reminds me of an afternoon last summer in The Osborne Village among the city freaks unemployed artists and musicians outside British pub on a patio up a few levels from the street, two friends with me, one very tall thin native guy long black ponytail streaked with gray halfway down his back same color beard, other very tall large-set skin-head looking fellow pierced eyebrow ears nose tongue Doc Martens an artist paints beautiful erotic shit, warm afternoon watching people cruise the busy street cars blowing their wads dangerous goth women in front of us vampire skin combat boots black lipstick fishnet stockings torn tights we comment to ourselves, we talk and laugh, bald guy just returned from a four year stint in New Orleans as a cook illegally owned his own restaurant for awhile, illegal driver's license, illegal security card, experienced the jazzy rain of New Orleans while it lasted then they caught him and booted his ass out of the grand ol' USA, ha ha who gives a damn he says America can go fuck itself, Native guy works for an environmental organization sails around the world for a living seen the whole fucking orb, been arrested twelve times in various countries for environmental actions, tree-hugging, hanging banners, barricading roads, driving dinghies in front of ocean liners all that stuff and more, just got in from Brazil says he's glad to be back home cuz nothing happens here, so we're trying to catch up in the shade under the sun tall blond walks down the street just below us, sees me and winks I wave at her beautiful ass moving away from me and get back to my Gin and Tonic, five seconds later she's coming up the steps big smile tight jeans looks like she slept in them gray shirt ruffled and stained big beautiful smile already drunk some drug in there too, sits right beside me begins talking without missing a beat -

"Hey, how are you boys? How are you crazy fuckers?"

We say something in return but she's focusing mainly on me doing the talk orders a Vodka/Orange telling me she just got out of jail for lifting some headphones from a record store was still drunk from the night before,

"Got fucked by two guys at the same time last night"

"I see"

"Met them at The Zoo"

"Surprise, surprise"

Bald friend starts talking to blond drunk seems interested chick pretty wired crazy showing us the form from the cops to prove she ain't bullshitting, she really is a pretty girl but I was turned off the second she opened her mouth, she's talking about her piercings Native friend rolling his eyes orders two more beers lights Turkish cigarette, she's showing us her pierced nipples now tits in full view while people walk up and down the street fully aware of the situation some even smiling, waiter making frequent trips to our table as woman shows us tits again and again, suddenly we're not so bored don't understand this, it's just a pair of breasts what the hell, but they're round and tanned huge nipples talking to me like Topo Gigio, also got stud in her tongue too many of these in my opinion fucking cops she's saying, fucking cops, Native guy now laughing his head off quiets down when her shirt goes up, bald guy intent on something I see wheels burning rubber in his head I'm playing with her nipple rings lightly she's smiling cooing like a cat, sign across the street says sushi-to-go,

"I'll fuck any one who gets me some sushi" she says,

"More beer" says Native guy

Tables all around us aware of loose-lips-sally no one embarrassed just cool drinking in The Village Saturday afternoon she's telling us her apartment just down the street off Corydon inviting us there we only have to "pay for the booze and some pot would be nice" has one more piercing on her vagina showing us right there at the table this time both my friends leaning way back for a better look tiny hoop slit right through light blond hairs looks almost delicate by now I'm making it clear we're not going to take turns fucking her, bald friend not so convinced, Native guy finds whole thing nothing but a gas, a big motherfucking ball he's laughing the moments away loose-lips-sally finally gets the point she's damn lucky we're not low-lifes, could have had our way with her and sliced her up, ripped off entire apartment, or was it her who was playing us? maybe some gangbangers at her apartment ready to slice and dice, who knows, either way very interesting, much drama flesh and sex alive and well, she takes off makes for The Zoo hard rock drinking joint if she's looking for trouble she'll find it there, back at the bar with the Chinese bartender he's got sister in hospital maybe terminal he's not talking about it whole story in his eyes, bus-stop-girl talking with Stripper casually putting her socks on shot of black Sambuca in front of me I take it in two small gulps, reporter's mother died six years ago lives with father good relationship a rare thing,

"How come I always see you here in the afternoons when you're supposed to be working?" I say,

"Are you still doing security work?"

"Listen, I fucking hate work, I hate working at any job for any period of time, anything that forces a schedule on me and takes away from MY free time is an enemy...it was the same with school, with University, with overbearing friendships...gotta find a way out man or it's curtains for me..."

"Don't know what to say, everyone hates work"

"I know, but it's different with me, this is an intense resentment...and I'm not naive or lazy and I don't expect anyone else to support me, I've done most of the shit jobs this society has to offer man"

"I know, we've talked about it"

"Lucky thing is I know how to hustle and take time off, work for a year, be a bum for a couple of months, work for two or three years, be a bum for another couple of months, you know"

"There's a price to pay for that lifestyle"

"I know it, the price you pay is you're going to be broke, you're going to lose apartments and have women leave you, and you have to be happy about it, anyone can walk around being bitter and pissed-off with empty pockets...but every time I go back to work I tell ya it gets harder and harder to smile...I would trade more leisure time for less money in my pocket anytime...there you go, my complete personal philosophy"

"At least you got one...listen, I haven't had any female contact in a long time"

"Nothing to worry about, it's overrated...how's your old man?"

"Good, good, went fishing with him last week...I've inherited his genetic thirst for alcohol"

I raise my glass,

"Who's this young woman you're with?"

"Well listen here music man..."

I tell him about the whole day with excitement speaking very fast which is my wont, he's got blue eyes scruffy beard dress pants loose red tie The Doors are coming from the jukebox, he listens nods smiles looks at bus-stop girl she joins us breathing a bit heavy has some beer lights a smoke rubs my arm without looking at me suggesting something is it sex? Not quite, more like affection or an acknowledgement of some kind, she likes her booze this rock and roll trixie, find myself wondering how she'll fare in time alcohol game being the most tricky of all if not careful the bottle will swallow you whole, another downtown flunky friend of reporter joins our table long ponytail blue baseball cap worn forwards this guy a scammer seen him around the neighborhood for years got drunk with him many times but always kept him at arm's length, he's shaking hands with slow-motion-girl "can anyone buy me a drink?" reporter says okay as he would scammer starts talking about his latest, he's married for money hates his wife only waiting for the allotted time when he can suck some cash out of her then he's splitting, he's got the whole table laughing cuz of that permanent wiry grin cigarette hanging from corner of mouth drinks Rye and coke paid by reporter bus-stop-girl not liking this guy too much I see clenched teeth through the laughter personally don't give a shit what they think of each other scammer guy not short on charm quite the good looking fellow in that rock and roll sense cheats on his wife like last day alive getting women no problem he's moved closer to bus-stop-girl sending out the signals she leans over says something in his ear he pulls back red-faced never seen such a sudden mood swing he's despondent moves his chair away from her we're doing a good job of pretending we didn't notice, I don't like hurting people's feelings for some stupid reason don't like the looks in their faces when I'm responsible for the sadness not cuz I'm a particularly kind man but just cuz I don't want the responsibility, she goes to the juke again blasts Nirvana into the room scammer guy talking crazy quiets down when she returns he's invisible to her as the clock keeps ticking vain attempts on his part to participate he's beaten man, whatever she said was a knockout punch, he leaves but not before bumming a few bucks off reporter who also splits after short time leaving me and my friend, her punk-rock smile in full bloom now, she crosses her legs, purses her lips, half full glass of beer in front of me, open Du Maurier pack on table three cigarettes left, group of loud drunks at the back, couple of gang members sit in the corner, few Filipino guys shoot the shit by the washroom, one passes another a piece of tinfoil, there's a beautiful black woman walking the bar cannonball ass right behind me, her reflection in the mirror on stage alluring somehow, my friend's turtleneck hugs her body showing off her breasts just right big round young full of fancy, volume in here at frenzy level song from "American Graffiti" comes on three Native women on stage doing the 1950's rock and roll dance tight jeans black boots crowd feeling the electricity making grooves girls doing shooters on this drunk-love Thursday night my friend's howling mad-dog run for your life hipster!

Love "American Graffiti", love American 1950's early sixties pop-culture the birth of rock and roll all the hipster poets hanging around drive-inn movies the thing from outer space creature from the black lagoon that sub-current teenage explosion blasting through the underground telling the mainstream and its cellophane wrapped philosophy to go fuck itself I figure the fifties was where my particular battle began, ideologically, us versus you and you know who you are, so I'm digging this moment watching the young girls shimmy to fifties rock and my friend shaking her thing hips like madness guitar buzzing in the ghetto manic guttersnipes orange phoenix twilight friend gets up moves towards back I start thinking of an old Deuce Coup with the engine sticking out of the hood, this is a miserable time we're living in, it's a paranoid and primitive society a fear culture spreading its disease further and further seems like those in charge want to do everything in their power to stop us from having a good time, when did this begin? When did we start counting calories and worrying about germs on the kitchen counter? Very sad sight to watch someone jogging down the street trying to fight off the inevitable decay of the human body, very sad indeed when wanting to be healthy is actually turned into a paranoid obsession, that's what all this smoke-ban stuff is about, if you listen to THEM just being in the proximity of cigarette smoke will kill you in the most horrendous of ways, I've considered quitting smoking many times (and one day I just might) for reasons of my own none of them to do with this recent tobacco witch-hunt just another symptom of a fear-gripped society bent on treating us like children determined not to let us experience anything mind altering even though our brains are hardwired to look for consciousness expanding experiences been that way since day one since that first primate somewhere in South America popped a peyote in his mouth and went oooooooh yeah, very funky, can anyone with half a brain wrap their head around the fact that marijuana is still illegal, prohibition doesn't work the 1920's proved that society's problems aren't due to drugs they're do to human beings, drugs don't create personalities they only make manifest what's already there, madmen, killers, psychopaths are everywhere man, let us normal folk smoke some grass every once in awhile drink some whiskey smoke a cigarette for fuck's sake, god forbid we should get any enjoyment out of this dreary convention-laden society that absolutely refuses to recognize human nature, seriously thought that battle was already won, I'm thinking of this completely surrounded by cigarette smoke my friend comes back with one hanging off her lips looking angry and tough very sensual when dark cloud above her doesn't want to talk which makes me happy seeing that I didn't really want to hear about it, not in the mood for dark clouds plenty of them in my life she sits quietly no more American Graffiti young dancing girls gone as well crowd thinning out unpleasant conversation all that's left she looks at me eyes asking questions, body language tightly wound something urgent on her mind, she waves it off and orders a drink seems she's still tripping another walk to the juke "Guns of Brighton" comes on we talk about whatever the hell we want to the backdrop of one of the greatest bands of all time in downtown Winnipeg going nowhere me and her nowhere man doing nothing, going nowhere...

We decide to walk for awhile incredibly warm out here considering it was deathly cold this afternoon, warm for The Peg in January that is, huge snowflakes still falling but very far apart coming down lazy slacker generation lazy I unzip my leather jacket we're walking down Albert Street in The Exchange District through the cobblestone the old buildings turn of the century architecture old warehouses of different colors red brick, orange, brown, yellow, streetlights short and black sort of Victorian style could almost pass for gaslight at a distance, few coffee-shops on the right underground cafe bookstore trendy nightclub and pish-posh restaurant, we're talking like we've known each other for ten thousand years and maybe we have,

"I thought I was the only one capable of drinking this hard and still being kinda coherent"

"You've met your match there sister Mary"

"Uh-huh, love this part of the city, looks like old Chicago with all the fire-escapes and warehouses..."

"Don't know if it's the booze or not, but how the hell did it get so warm?"

"It's not just the booze, look at those guys over there"

A couple of young guys walk parallel to us across the street wearing jean jackets and runners, they're laughing and seem happy,

"Wonder what those punks are up to tonight"

"Pretty much the same thing we are I'll bet"

"Listen, what Canadian movies have you liked?"

"Saw this movie on Bravo called 'Last Night' with-"

"-Don Mckellar, pretty intense stuff"

"Yeah, the end was hard to watch, in a good sense I mean"

"You make a decent living from selling pot?"

"I scrounge a living, but beats the shit out of regular work, don't you think?"

"You have no idea how much I agree with you...used to sell pot myself, ended up smoking more than I was selling"

"That's the trick man, self-control"

We're now at Old Market Square an urban park with a cement stage four or five steps high under a canopy pillars on either side few coffee shops across the street

British pub fancy restaurant on corner in summer
bands play here for the Jazz Festival everyday at noon,
used to sit on the grass after a joint listen to the sounds
watch the pretty girls in their jean shorts and cultured
assholes,

"Let's light up" she says,

We spark it up passing it back and forth under the
funky streetlights Artspace building right in front of us
that's where artists rent rooms to practice their plays or
read their scripts or jerk-off in the moonlight for all I
care, also independent movie theatre on first floor,
brought many a failed relationship there watching the
great art film unfold as our connection withered away
turning to shit-in-the-face for reasons unknown,

"So I'm thinking" I say "I'd like to buy that gram of
hash you were talking about"

She goes into her pocket without hesitation hands it to
me,

"A thank you for the kind of day we've experienced"

"Well I think I'll take it, thank you very much, not
easy to find hash these days"

"It's from the East Coast, a gift from my dear
boyfriend, the last one I'll bet"

"I'll bet"

"Are you making fun of me?"

"No, you kidding? Please continue"

"You wouldn't want to move to the East Coast, would you?"

"No, but why are you asking?"

"Just wondering how tied up you are to this city"

"I'm not interested in many other places, a few cities of the world intrigue me like I've said, but that's about it, certainly don't want to live anywhere else at the moment...probably someday I'll live someplace else, don't know, don't care"

"I'm trying to understand that philosophy, but I've traveled my entire life, it's hard for me"

"I always get that same look when I tell people I don't like to travel, that stunned look like I've said something sacrilegious, it's all to do with having a personal philosophy in life, I refuse to seek out adventure, I refuse to think about how much better other places are cuz there's always someplace better, when adventure comes my way I deal with it how I see fit"

"Meaning?"

"Meaning, grab it by the horns, or get the fuck out of the way...depends how late I am for happy hour"

"Well aren't you special"

"I've had some crazy-ass experiences, believe me, enough to write ten novels, sold my chapbooks at downtown bars and on the streets right out of my knapsack, you know, around Hargrave and Kennedy, Ellice all that..."

"Is that why so many people know you?"

"Partly, and it's not so many"

"I was wondering if there was a bartender that DIDN'T know what you drank in the downtown area"

"Anyway, I'm not afraid of experience, that should be pretty fucking clear after today, right?"

"Well, you lost your job to follow the vibe, so I'd say so"

"Traveling is for suckers"

"Being a smart ass again"

"I'm just tired of the same reaction to the same questions, people are so fucking predictable"

"Are you calling me predictable?"

"No, not you, sorry, you're an angel with a cigarette"

"Good back tracking buddy...don't worry, I share your cynicism about people"

"It's not that I don't like people, I'm not Bukowski sticking my reverse snobbery drunken nose up in the air, I like people, I just don't trust them, and in order to continue liking them I have to limit my time around them...I'm not a total recluse but the tendencies are there"

"I can see that, yet people seem to like you"

"I don't know why that is...anyway the same can be said about you"

"Never had a problem meeting people, never hung out with the popular group either, but never been alone unless I wanted to be...tell me about your band, what were you guys like?"

"I'm pretty drunk, how about you?"

"Yeah, don't know how long this coherent thing will last"

"Juicy"

"Check out those dark clouds"

"How about that building?"

"Which one?"

"See, in the back there, with the red bricks and the steam coming out of the stack"""

"Nice"

"Look, there's a line-up at that cheesy nightclub"

"Let's go spit on them"

"Don't joke, five years ago I would have done it"

"Same here"

"Follow me"

"Yes master"

"Did you see The Hoodoo Gurus at The Playhouse Theatre?"

"When was that?"

"Few years ago"

"Wasn't living here..."

"Man, what a show that was...from that first chord on all I felt was wild-drunk-happy..."

"Your favorite gig?"

"That and a few others...nothing better than The Pixies of course"

"Hey, I was there too, where were you sitting?"

"Ten rows from the front, great fucking performance..."

"Rock and roll gets no better than that, no better"

"No fucking better, no way, no how..."

The Pixies foremost on our mind we share concert experiences though concert wrong word far more intimate than that maybe 1000 people close enough to see Kim Deal fuck-up on the bass with that brilliant dum-du-dum-dum that she does better than anyone beautiful Walker Theatre with the opera booths up top on either side large chandeliers all faces from the past just a little older now young enough to still rock the casbah real young punks there as well seems my friend was up in the booth on Kim Deal's side, saw Kim chugging the beers chain smoking the Marlboros rock and roll in the true sense, unassuming, scars and all, Frank Black genius song writer one three-chord eccentric riff after the other,

"Did your band sound anything like that?"

"No, more like The Replacements but with a blues background, they used to call us punk-blues"

"Juicy"

"Let's go this way"

Through the warehouses sound of music coming from certain windows bands renting large lofts to play it loud, drums echo under the streetlights, someone howls in the distance, two more howls a few laughs, neon shop on the right like an acid trip, warehouse up ahead sells furniture, Chinese restaurant hugs street corner small patio circles the front, ornate street-bench on every block passed out under that one there once, my friend talking about everything she sees taking in the entire thing with a relaxed excitement footsteps in the snow one after the other I remember waking up to the sound of a delivery truck backing up in the alley wallet still in back pocket I was alright, hot sun beating on my head walking home every step momentous pain in legs guts melting asshole screaming, ride it out till next time let it come I say, on with the bullshit got my friend piggyback feeling the bottom of the thighs in my hands the fat and the muscle my cock extending she's laughing about something I ignore her arms around my neck faint whiff of perfume in my ear along with cigarette smoke and alcohol she's by my side again young punk with bomber jacket here too he's asking for a smoke we give him one shoot the shit for awhile kid moves on down the street hands cupped army boots sliding sees car slowly idling hunches down and grabs hold of back bumper goes for a bumper-shine car takes off kid in tow,

"Crazy Osborne Village punk"

"I told you I'm living there, right?" she says,

"Yeah"

"I like the way it feels now, just the right mix of derelicts and artists"

"Same fucking thing, derelict and artist"

"I mean real derelicts, moron, not mohawk kid on the corner"

"Got ya"

"It used to be too trendy a few years ago, seems to have toughened up"

"That's cuz of The Zoo"

"Crazy-ass fucking place, my friend tells me it used to be a biker bar"

"Hung out there when it was, they wore their colors right in the fucking bar, snorted coke on the table, whatever the fuck they wanted..."

"Did you party with them?"

"Hardly ever, went to a few parties at their clubhouse"

"Must have been wild"

"Sure, just another scene, avoid the violence and you're alright"

"Would you go to a party if I invited you?"

"What do you mean, a house party?"

"Yes"

"No, I hate house parties"

"Okay"

"I'll go somewhere else with you though"

"Oh, is that right?"

"Smart girl, keep talking"

"Wanna smoke?"

"Sure...thanks for everything, aah..."

I take the cigarette light it feeling slight hint of guilt she follows suit shakes her hips sound of frozen waterfalls prairie winter isolation not best thing I'm told by lumberjack trailor park boy front teeth missing baseball cap filthy sweatpants my friend's hips are curved like the autobahn and the mountains of Sicily she sucks on that smoke Ziggy's cigar and all the rest of the phallic Catholics under a pitch black sky not a star in sight she moves with mad grace got big feet big ass leaving sexual disaster in her wake slow-mo-girl easy groove melting into the sidewalk, I'm beside her got own nervous thing happening nervous energy like a halo follow the mandala man (circle represents integrity) broken whiskey bottle in my living room last cigarette a thing of madness grew up happy nothing but green grass or frozen winters either way remaining pure suave luck, I read Robert Crumb amidst new direction thinking rye and 7 too sweet beer too damn slow death hanging on thin wire I remember going to school in Gassino, Italy, 14 years of age girls looking different to me Canadian chicks not so refined at a glance discovered rock and roll through older brother lived in village up in the hills outside big city of Torino, walked downhill to school and uphill to home cemetery first then narrow street wound upwards for half an hour past tiny homes and apartments everything made of bricks and cement final leg steep gravel road that lead to my house surrounded by green hills and forest mountains just a touch away, sexy neighbor my age same school as me name of Fiorenza sat in her yard in jean-shorts on hot afternoons as we hurled profanities at each other from across the fence obviously in love...the hills of northern Italy, strange memory that one,

"Do you like comics?"

"What, comedians?" she says,

"No, no, comic books"

"Not much...I did like the movie 'American Splendor' though"

"That's a great comic, one of the heavyweights"

"They just don't do anything for me"

"It does seem to be a guy thing"

"Yes"

"Wonder why?"

"I think all that superhero macho shit detracts from the other more artistic stuff"

"Well I don't know if that makes any sense...however, you should read Love and Rockets, it's one of the best things I've ever read, and that includes literature"

"Sex..."

"...Do we have any booze or anything?"

"Flask was empty long time ago...we're approaching the Albert so hang on you old drunk"

Looking back Chinatown visible end of Exchange District beginning of ghetto ahead approaching crowd in front of cafe big group of people hanging out guys doing the feats of strength thing pushing each other sumo style all in friendly jest good-time departure from day to day asshole burn, people with beer in hand cheering talking looks like everyone knows each other punk goth alternative-rock along with the plain ugly and detached kind of scene don't like crowds anymore but day started at bus-stop will continue to logical conclusion my friend already in conversation with punk rock girl head shaved on the side rest of hair long and green pierced nose mouth tongue eyebrow whatever else I just kind of hang back cheering gets louder one guy falls back into snow winner comes forth looks like big college kid helps loser up I'm thinking it's a bit too civilized, no?

I tell myself it's a good thing for people to be happy, my friend moving away laughing hard feeling home moving closer I remain internally separate from whole thing liking my objective view feeling happy in the shadows talking the talk they listen as always even when my mind is detached young goth woman staring at me with dislike University couple ask questions as I tell stories of where I live crazy high-rise core-area withdrawals whorehouse on the corner, ha ha ha they say, uh-huh oh yeah, crack central man gangs running all over the streets people getting jacked for nothing but a case of beer girlfriend of mine arm busted in back alley behind beer vendor, all told in dark humor grin brain juice running University alt-rocker asks what I do, tell him I'm security guard bus-stop-girl comes out of nowhere "he's a writer, a published one" so I tell them what I write now we're suddenly talking about me in that small dark corner rest of crowd eyes on sumo shit big boys got nothing to prove I move aside cuz I want to let them talk things out manage to snag a beer from someone take a seat on a steel rail just slightly away from the rest watching steam blow out of my mouth winter air feeling crisp in my lungs cools the throat, my bus-stop-friend with rosy cheeks watching her talk to someone beautiful sight she smokes with black leather gloves I think we're all drunk out here, we're all high and drunk and lost and tired and sick of the whole fucking thing piss-poor ambition should play hooky on life more often as we laugh and laugh happy in the moment, she talks easy reluctant drunk-fuck plenty she moves as blue velvet on your thighs, puts a beer to her lips golden swallow follows anarchy in your living room, distant sirens her head turns left springs back tongue out ruby lips frozen in kiss kiss bang bang she says first thing in the morning plays hard heavy distant legs in the air a punk riff minor chord stiletto on the pavement, she glides clumsy-sensual word to word, legs like tombstone anacondas eyelashes dragonfly broken teeth on kitchen floor, I watch her hips move silent thunder she knows how the song goes man, it goes like this...

Husker Du was a great band so was Pink Floyd and Elvis Costello knew his stuff Tom Waits writes music like no other The Replacements did the indie rock thing about as good as it can be done but this is all yesterday, seems we're at a loss today, where are the artists? The writers, the musicians, the comic-book artists? Where's Michelangelo or Mozart or Joe Strummer or Robert Crumb? What kind of a world is this where something like 'Friends' could garner so much attention?

"What are you thinking about?" she says,

"Nothing at all, what's up?"

"See those guys over there?"

"With the blond chick?"

"Yeah, they're in a band, playing The Albert tonight, pretty interesting people"

"And what?"

"You up for some street drinking?"

"They got the booze?"

"Of course, c'mon..."

I follow meet these young people blond woman very tall about 5'10" or 5'11" towers over us large cans ass a bit flat wears cowboy hat other two guys young closely-cropped hair wearing bomber jackets dock martins, it's obvious woman the leader we're following them to one of the many tunnels in the Exchange District under an arched entrance connecting one street to another broken bottles and garbage everywhere we stand under the brick canopy watching the snow fall at each entrance, they're passing king cans of beer and a joint around woman annoying with her insistence on talking about herself so I focus on the guys asking about their music one kind of shy the other talkative seems like a good kid woman with my friend few feet away from us these guys in a punk band of course, nothing else at The Albert, they seem to know the older bands Bad Brains, The Addicts, DOA and so on with the wild pretensions never stop thinking, never compromise, don't eat the yellow snow said the man, punk rock not my favorite form of music but it's up there, one of the guys still lives with parents says he hates them, hates school and work you're on the right track I tell him, live with your folks as long as you can, I was well into my twenties when I moved out for the final time fully completely, seem to be getting along with these suburban punk rock kids feel young electricity going through me, still young I tell myself, still time, what's with the blond? I say pointing, she's the bass player writes all the songs,

"Also into mild domination"

"Inflicting or receiving?" I say,

"The former"

"Juicy"

Every so often someone walks by the entrance sees us and keeps moving I'm wondering why something like this would be against the law, see no harm in sitting around drinking beer talking laughing why should the law give a fuck? The women now with us my friend sticking close I feel her arm touching mine occasionally her tits rubbing against me this whole surreal fucking trip germinating in my mind, moon three quarters full layer of snow on the sidewalks buildings red orange yellow touch of green and neon tunnels all over the place arched entrances saying "come on in baby and I'll slit your throat", we're standing in a circle talking at the same time I'm aware of the symbolic significance, broken bottle of Rye in the corner, pair of underwear on top of old work boots, magazine on ground woman on cover half-naked, young punks pissing in the corner, can't escape that urine smell for some reason in downtown Winnipeg north of Portage it comes and goes randomly, still very beautiful just part of urban living jackass! hear the cement under your shoes the sirens out your window, pain in the ass kid begging for quarters sun up high in the prairie sky he plays a flute watch out cuz he digs it and you don't, don't know what to say about India but the drunken roar of right-here-right-now is all around me, girl with cowboy hat talks about her bass playing fellow band members spin around say oooh-yeah acting punk and it's okay, slow-motion-girl never too far gives me the okay sign time for another she says our hosts supply the booze young kids talk to me cowboy hat talks with my friend feeling real good out here wondering about nothing cuz I said so and no other reason...

When you're in full swing IT happens, forward momentum a reality no bullshit philosophy here keep head down focused on pace most important thing in life movies literature if pace is wrong whole thing falls apart, head down I seem to notice things, head up I go blind, politics no damn good people accept one lie after the other just part of whole thing, Democracy only works for the rich other methods no better, Communism is a farce ain't nothing more removed from human nature, we all know how shitty dictatorships are without ever living under one, anarchy would spell the end of the human race, primitive living hunters and gatherers too much damn physical labor, communes can kiss my ass, very little harmony to be found anywhere unless you make it man, almost entirely up to you, gasoline alley lit up like fireworks neon starlight gutter sleep face to face with God himself bored and idle Papa loads the barrel takes a shot down goes the elephant ensuring you'll never understand, white trash racist worst thing in the world everyone fallible everyone the same hate spills over tears your guts out streets drenched in blood cockroaches in your underwear you'll never destroy them, boy hates girl hates boy ain't nothing sacred wrong turn was taken somewhere down the line maybe future will be sparkling reality diverse ideas all accepted cobras and monkeys playing cards in outer space people driving their Chevys to the moon but I doubt it, extraterrestrial bums cigarettes on Hargrave and Cumberland Canadian Prime Minister hitchhiking to Mars wipes his ass with the lot of us story unfinished acid flashbacks inevitable guitar-sex groupie go for the quick fuck while you can...cowboy girl and myself still haven't said more than two words to each other which suits me fine got nothing to say to her arrogance in voice huge turn-off, arrogant moody people among worst on the planet, don't give a damn how good smart tough you are disrespect me and we got a problem, used to have more patience with people now not so much desire to mingle waning still refusing to give in to hate and all-out despair realizing the cruelty of the world has touched others far deeper than myself blessed by simple geography could easily be living on other side of planet among the truly starving, beer in one hand cigarette in other must have been born like this out of tune with society, in tune with bigger picture, used to practice guitar four or five hours a day in my mother's basement ready for the week-end gig never had stage-fright playing seedy bars all over town long-term girlfriend deep in the middle of it remember thinking she was the one engaged by the age of 20 truly a strange thing still friends to this day, singer and myself wrote the songs kicking ass heavy and loose partying hard living the life for five or six years on stage best feeling but disillusioned with the rock and roll business very early on began writing sporadic short stories then got the bug man and here we are, but those rock and roll days unforgettable and wild even at the small time level I was at (never went on tour) knew guy with philosophy degree took acid like candy he groovy with mind trip acrobatics talking till the sun came up we tripped out like we thought we were supposed to discussing Freud and Jung, Hendrix and Pink Floyd, Sid Vicious and Deborah Harry, Dylan Thomas and Alex Harvey (cute chick in aisle three she got jungle-ass) Kant and Henry Miller (woman at the back African eyes legs like suicide hanging) Hunter Thomson and Keith Richards, mainstream comics and the underground I'll have another please, women came around of course guitar around your neck for some reason all that's needed to get laid but none of this means shit so don't make that your raison d'être art is the thing or should be, gust of wind flies through tunnel old newspaper hits bus-stop-girl in head large target with that funky mushroom cloud we're all laughing see crowd on street thinning get back out to the world everyone moving towards the bar looks like quite the scene no lack of good music in this town my friend hangs back tugging at my jacket,

"Let's go there for a second" she says,

Small diner with barstools facing large windows looking out at the street,

"What about the bar?"

"Just for a minute, okay?"

"No problem"

I follow her to the front door large no-smoking sign on it few downtown flunkies scattered across the place teenage girl behind counter take a stool stare out window hear my friend order two cokes then she goes to the washroom feel the cold air through the window everything white and gray and streetlight-orange, occasional person walking hunched over mostly empty streets, dead streets, snow mixes with gravel and mud turns into brown filth can't avoid it all winter long buses most disgusting shit's had all day to melt sticks to your shoes then your shoes take it someplace else, in winter seen from above city sparkles layer of pearl white over everything down at street level things jagged violent exciting dangerous during the day kids play on snow mountains at night only the insane wander the streets looking for another drink in dark corners whiskey suicide youth gang vibration winter isolation makes Johnny play guitar boy...hey, she says, here, I take the coke she sits beside me realize there's Rye in there before it touches my mouth she must have gotten it from those kids we were drinking with she winks nice swallow sugar whiskey down the gullet, gust of wind picks up blows snow down the street for some reason we smile,

"Winter seen from indoors is amazing" she says,

"Sometimes, yeah..."

"Life hasn't been as easy for me as you might think"

"I never thought that"

"You, I see the trouble in your eyes...on your face...you've been fucked over...despite it, you're happy"

"Don't know if that's the right word...not even sure if I know what it means"

"So what do you think of me?"

"What's not to like?"

"Do you like science fiction?" she says laughing,

"On film, not in literature, uhhh..."

"Don't like to imagine things or what?"

"Funny, really, believe me...they're usually written in that typical, normal prose that explains every single character in extreme detail as soon as they're introduced, his brother came from here, his mother was a space-whore, blah and blah bullshit, far to dry, no sense of art at all...but on the screen I can handle bad dialogue, in fact the badder the better, bad script, bad acting, actually there's an art to making a bad science fiction movie, not many can do it..."

"I think I know what you mean, but I'm not sure..."

Two older guys at the front counter drunk as hell arguing about something too stupid to mention get into it start grabbing each other's coats and faces one holding a bag of chips the other's jacket only half-on one sleeve in other guy's hands girl behind counter giving the occasional "hey!" "what the!" other people in place look sad distant my friend standing up I sit back cuz this fucking thing is hilarious, why does no one see it, it's fucking hilarious, why the sadness, who gives a fuck? Thing continues slowly winds down I'm already looking out the window before it's over old drunks seem to disappear quickly of course everyone starts talking about it before my friend can say anything I start up,

"Ya think Superman could take The Hulk?"

"'Blade Runner' was, I believe, the best film ever made...that's why I asked you about science fiction..."

"Did you read 'Do Androids Dream of Electric Sheep'?"

"Sure, several times...you can't say that's not good writing"

"It is, just meant that it's rare in that genre"

"It's rare in every genre"

I think about that one conclude she's right,

"I understand good manners" she says "but political correctness is bullshit, I can't believe people actually buy into that thinking it's some kind of solution...basically they're asking you to lie cuz somehow it'll get better that way..."

"It all started in the fucking nineties, it's a bucket of shit"

"The nineties were fucking horrible!"

"There were only three good things in the nineties – "

"-You're too generous"

"Alternative rock, and that was only at the beginning, basketball, and Quentin Tarantino"

"Right on brother"

"What bothers me even more about today is everyone pretending to be so open-minded, everyone!"

"How do you mean?"

"You know, everyone's afraid to insult someone or some group so they pretend everything on the face of the planet has merit, you know, people that say stuff like - all forms of music are equally valid, it's all about personal taste...yeah well, know what I say, you can like whatever the fuck you want but don't be telling me Britney Spears is just as valid as Tom Waits, got it?...there's a definition of quality going on here..."

"And who decides what's quality?"

"Ahh, you see, nobody decides, it just IS, either you see it or you don't"

"Really?"

"Yeah, Hemingway vs. Tom Clancy, you tell me? Bukowski vs. Stephen King? The Ramones vs. Styx? Basketball vs. Curling?"

"But what if someone said Shakespeare vs. Poe?"

"They both got it, at that point it's a matter of taste"

She rolls her eyes,

"If you ask someone what kind of me music they like and their reply is 'all kinds', take that as a red flag man, tell them to fuck off"

"I feel like I should shout out to the neighborhood 'ANY QUESTIONS?'" she says pointing her hands at me,

"Watch Lexx if you like science fiction"

"Heard about it"

"Well have you heard about the Three Color trilogy?"

"Of course, what the fuck's that got to do with science fiction?"

"I seem to recall you saying you liked European movies"

"Yeah well, that Three Color trilogy is some of the best filmmaking you're ever going to see, period"

"No argument here, that's some powerful shit"

"So you like art movies or what the fuck?"

"I like them...it's just that one type that pisses me off, those real boring three hour soul-searching movies...like Godard, all those long pauses and static shots...you know, art films are tricky, you have to walk that line between something of quality and something pretentious, and let's face it nobody with a brain wants pretentious"

"That's what really bugs me about this part of the world, anything that is even remotely artistic or intelligent is labeled as pretentious...not enough car crashes and fight scenes I suppose"

"That's American movies you're talking about, Canadian movies are as artistic as you can get...without boring the shit out of someone"

"Boring the shit out of someone?"

"Let's face it, art can get boring, you need a bad movie once in awhile, c'mon, what the fuck"

"Who's your favorite filmmaker?"

"Fellini...maybe Woody Allen or David Lynch, one of those guys"

"I thought you might say Russ Myers..." she laughs,

"Hey, he was great"

"I wonder if you would say that if you were a woman"

"Look, his is a male perspective, he's a man, what do you expect?"

"Back off man, I happen to like Russ Myers movies"

"Sure, whatever..."

I'm sucking Rye and coke through a straw like a teenager my friend beside me at times looks barely out of her teens she's quiet sipping booze looks out window looks down at her boots I'm looking around wandering mind elsewhere seeing colors and shapes form tight circles then fade slowly green river red sand octopus smile shards of flesh frozen solid in the wasteland energy ice-pond Gods leaving Vegas I'm aware of my friend beside me aware of her figure shrouded in black mouthing the words "it's okay...it's okay..." she leans back beside me casually lights a smoke and looks around, teenage employee sees her says nothing goes back to magazine, couple at table glance over entirely uninterested turn away, she leans her head against me takes a puff in the no-smoking-zone, my arm is around her, we're looking out the window, snow is blowing down the street, old guy under streetlight slips on a patch of ice, woman at bus-stop crosses her arms, wind blows through cracks in the window my friend passes me the cigarette and I stare straight ahead...

The night is alive they say we walk through the front door full punk crowd out skin-heads mohawks army boots everywhere couple of long-hairs here as well a touch of the working class it's draft night at The Albert we order the cheap draft three chord music coming from large speakers owner tending bar my friend immediately spots someone she knows tall girl in black tights black hair purple streaks I move away find a seat close to the bar about to start talking to long-hair beside me first band comes on tears into a rockabilly-punk tune they got the sideburns and leather jackets stand-up drums really kicking it I'm up front with my friend moving somewhat to the music feel a mosh-pit forming decide to move away my friend grabs my arm,

"WHERE ARE YOU GOING?"

"WHAT, CAN'T HEAR YOU..."

"WHERE ARE – "

"- DON'T LIKE MOSH-PITS, I'LL BE AT THE BAR"

"COOL"

I move my 38 year old ass back to the bar and start talking to a woman I used to know everything fine in tune with the rockabilly overtures and 50 cent draft, we're close to the same age went to abnormal psychology with her during my University years she's carrying a camera has some kind of press badge my friend lost somewhere in the mosh-pit she's kicking her heels punk-rockers beware, University girl standing on barstool big round thighs and ass by my face taking pictures of the band head full of liquor and academia, room always full on draft nights got a girl in thigh-highs circling the bar leather corset big tits, guy by sound booth looks like Jim Morrison drinking Blue smoking Players Light, girlfriend with him dark circles under her eyes passes a joint looking nervous and guilty, couple of skin-heads cruise the bar territorial-like they're loud and large and they scare me none, pinball machines lit up at the back group of mohawks hangs there beautiful colors in their spikes leather jackets with Sex Pistols stickers on them, been coming to this bar for almost twenty years off and on damn lousy beautiful place hasn't changed a bit feels lost but alright, my friend comes back to me breathing heavy puts her arm around mine we shout in the insanity she says,

"HOLD ON, I'LL BE RIGHT BACK"

Watch her walk away love the ass receding from view with that particular jiggle bounce it hard and fast really nice piece of work see her go around corner to front re-focus on bar eyes moving from side to side it is packed shoulder to shoulder small pockets of room only the veteran knows, usually a barstool or by the sound-man, sometimes the pool table has some space once games are done, you can always lean against the pinball machine looking clumsy-cool, back of bar far from the stage by VLT's always empty, one side of wall is large mirrors remember coming here on acid 18 or 19 years old thinking this was huge place almost walked into mirror, never liked those fucking things, bartender owner's son talks to me about something I smile say "sure, oh yeah" he's a big motherfucker wouldn't want to mess with him but don't give a damn cuz he's a good fellow and I'm 85% pacifist, the other 15% watch out man it's the killing joke...my band played here in 1989 rocked the joint with our punk-blues though I sensed the crowd wasn't too keen on all the lead guitar stuff, my understanding being punkers hate lead guitar, all too stupid, all too elitist, good songs are good songs lead guitar or not, play the fiddle, the accordion, the trumpet, the tiny hairs coming out of your ass I repeat, good songs are good songs, avoid the poseur musical masturbation if possible (Yes, Led Zeppelin, Jethro Tull, Genesis, Rush, Deep Purple, The Eagles, Black Sabbath, Uriah Heep, U2, Van Halen, 80's hair-bands, Lenny Kravitz, Status Quo, Styx, etc.) it can be harmful to the psyche if taken in large doses, here comes my friend through the crowd I swear I feel the waves of something wild she clumsily makes room for herself some move aside others remain the assholes they will always be, I'm by the bar she stands by me...my eyes on her's look like tears,

"I JUST CALLED MY BOYFRIEND..."

"OKAY, AND..."

"I BROKE UP WITH HIM..."

"WHAT'S THAT?"

"WHAT?"

"I DIDN'T HEAR YOU"

"I BROKE UP WITH HIM"

"OH, AHH..."

We kinda look around uh-huh okay rockabilly-punk band does final song to outsider music still loud seems almost a whisper to us now someone I know pops up alright buddy, we're talking all three of us drunk as hell but still okay talking to the rhythm of the room nothing important all too easy meaningless but no need to infuse all things with deep meaning cuz loco character round the block he's crazy and cool and unafraid like fire electricity and solar energy destruction this guy slightly balding around my age rock and roll intelligent bus-stop girl into him seems almost sexual maybe imagination insecurity psyche alive healthy tells me not to give a damn don't really give a damn about nothing, interesting tunes on the speakers some garage 60's rock even surf stuff with the tremolo guitar chord we're talking all equal, no worries for the moment, no unconscious desire full surface rising got telescope hangover catch a bus on Graham and Carlton skater kids electra gliding blue young African woman in jean-shorts white runners her friend Oriental tilts from side to side she's got the groove black sandals painted toenails cop car eases forward young student rollerblades down hot summer cement thighs so long like a snake tattoo sunlight New Orleans easy shuffle crime gone rampant more like easy killing small things down fire-escape back alley knife at your throat night on the prairies clearing in the middle of bush and forest easy friends talking by trailer sky nothing but stars man dog running wild couple of chicks barefoot in the grass tight shorts ain't no other we're passing joints under the milky way beer is everywhere maybe some meaning in all this most likely just shooting hoops at midnight I look over to my friend hoping for wisdom and say "gotta beer?" "sure" "too many mosquitoes" "no doubt" country air not so good route your mind back to this fucking bar drunk spills beer on my jacket falls over my friend starts yelling,

"No, no" I say "No problem"

"Fucking idiot!" she says

I look at the guy he's completely wasted not meaning any harm written all over his face I feel extreme pity for the man bartender grabs him by shirt starts dragging poor bastard out the door look of complete confusion on guy's face probably went out for a good time never thought the gutter would be his bed for the night, maybe he's lucky drunk-tank doors always open, what the hell, it's winter...

Place is on edge large crowds and alcohol never a good mix but it's always been like this never saw much bullshit here, saw guy hit girlfriend in head with a chair at another downtown bar once, saw other guy get thrown out glass window, shot the shit with ex-con large gash on throat he got in jail alright guy been through hell and then some, this crowd more that young punk rock thing though some heavies are here, not oldest one in room but pretty damn close I slide over to the sound-man a bit of space to lean up against the wall light a smoke my friend beside me we're talking intently about our lives while the surroundings go out-of-control madness dance floor is packed no mosh-pit people just standing around talking holding their beers to their chests trying to look cool distant we're flirting heavier now everything out in the open just inches apart bodies always touching ever so slightly she sees a couple of barstools open up takes me there by the hand orders two Rye and 7's she takes a sip kisses me straight on the lips waiting for my reaction what's a man to do?

"I'm single now, I feel fucking great" she says,

"I know that feeling"

"Do you think maybe we should talk or something?..I mean..."

"Listen, I..."

Move in give her a kiss taste the alcohol on her lips moist and warm got my hand in that massive hair feeling her curls slip through my fingers and it continues...

Second band comes on she jumps up says she's going to the dance floor good solid rock and roll band with shades of punk no mosh-pit but floor packed to the distorted buzzsaw guitar drummer possessed wild beat sledgehammer solid everyone doing the whiskey-jig my friend's head bopping up from the crowd like a magic mushroom, feel hand on my shoulder reporter friend back large smile on his face he saddles up seems he was cruising the strip joints a lot happier now he buys me a drink I see the band we were drinking with outside by the pinball machines cowboy girl towering over everyone still not entirely convinced she's not a tranny, a sexy one at that, band really kicking it long time since I heard something of this caliber short explosive songs guitar bursts bass dumm-dumm doing a Ska song now whole room feeling it from the pool tables to the front bar everyone moving, got big smile on my face lighting one cigarette after the other reporter waves people to our table lady with gray hair, very tall blond big hips early twenties, guy in his mid-thirties long greasy hair, regulars here but part of the day crowd, old drunks from hotel upstairs, downtown workers and scammers, sometimes they spill over into the night too drunk to give a fuck but still the pros able to navigate any bar any time, they don't mix with the night crowd and vice-versa, gray-haired lady is actually complaining about the loud music,

"What are you still doing here?" I say,

"My bar, baby"

"You're one hell of a woman"

"I'll fuck you silly"

My friend back from dance floor sits beside me we have to do some serious seat shuffling to accommodate her she acts like it's all normal she's got it coming somehow and she's right, tall blond seems to like her but gray-haired lady doesn't I couldn't care less cuz I'm really into the band hear my table arguing in the background keep my focus on the stage, three Ska songs in a row now they're into a rock and roll riff bassist shaved head with long beard down his front tied in a knot at the end hitting those notes like John Entwistle he's running up and down the neck still precision timing with the drums and the guitar loudest thing as it should be, voice like gravel singing songs of rebellion always in style, my friend arguing with gray-haired lady but nothing violent almost playful these jokers too drunk for anything anyway, see cowboy girl doing some air-guitar gyrations her band-mates smiling in awe, reporter friend enjoying whole thing why he can't get a woman still a deep mystery to me strange city strange reality, if you let yourself go entirely watch mind move through the fabric you get a very slight hint of what might actually be going on around you, forget what you've been told especially in grade school (don't listen to doctors, lawyers, scientists, real estate agents, Margaret Atwood, environmentalists, shopkeepers, New

York chefs, teachers, university professors, politicians or philosophers) very few absolute truths let the unconscious mind go where it will answers are there not in classrooms, the people who profess to save the world are the ones to watch out for don't know exactly why I never trusted that lot but something doesn't sit right, band running wild I'm talking to gray-haired lady she's smiling looks over at my friend and frowns then looks at me smiles again my friend's eyebrows pointing downwards like Satan other long-hair at table just sitting back quiet either too drunk or making plans I decide then and there if fucker gets violent my pacifism is out the window, band finishes song immediately goes into next one I like when bands do that no need for all that bullshit talk HELLO WINNIPEG just crank it up play the tunes this ain't no spoken word crap, goddamn my friend gets into it again with gray-hair can't hear what the hell the problem is but starting to bother me I move to the bar my friend follows immediately she's beside me mouthing the word "sorry" I wave it off lick her forearm concentrate on the band heads bopping girl in black tights large powerful thighs thin waist dyed bright red hair in front of me doing the alt-jig beautiful powerful sexy sight guy beside her moron looks like heavy metal type bandana tight jeans Van Halen hair, other guy pops up out of nowhere knows my friend asks her to dance off they go I order another Scotch pay with the $20.00 she gave me, even-steven my man, notice bartender arguing with waitress a few tables down from me he whispers in her ear she picks up chair and throws it at him hits top of his legs owner right there they're mixing it up, hardly anyone notices this everything too loud power chords shaking the foundations entire front section of bar glued to the stage who are these punks I wonder, thinking about this book I'm reading by Carl Jung called "Memories, Dreams, Reflections" have to remember to suggest it to bus-stop-girl as punk rocker does a stage dive, like watching a freak circus man find myself laughing out loud almost spill young woman's drink beside me "sorry sorry" "alright" she says turns to the stage, there's one stage dive after the other and this is the point when things get shitty I say get off the fucking stage let the band play, spoken like a man approaching his forties faster than he would like several people in the room my age or older seem to ignore the stage altogether University girl with cannonball ass up front taking pictures, her ass tilts to one side then the other thighs follow suit leaning forward then backward tits like wildfire mega-bombs hair swinging round and round unaware my eyes follow every movement, she's in black underwear in my apartment early afternoon she's looking out my huge floor-to-ceiling windows large thighs too beautiful to describe toes painted aqua velvet tiny tank-top barely holds in her breasts aching to pop out like ripe watermelons nipples large and pink, she's leaning forward, she's passing me an orange juice, we're both hungover talking about books and movies and small miracles, then she's gone into the crowd a lesson to be learned another kid stage dives song kicks into a double beat my friend comes out of the crowd almost in slow motion altogether beautiful young crazy, she's catching her breath chest heaving in and out love that turtleneck leans back slips it off black tank-top underneath shoves shirt into her parka first time I see her long arms natural Native tan well-built in the no-work-out sense few bracelets on her wrists one made of leather watch with Minnie Mouse face cover, she looks directly into my eyes smiles orders two more drinks I've noticed she's slowed down since coming in here busy on the dance floor maybe sensed herself going a bit too far but I dig women who know how to drink, no better drinking session than with a woman in a small smoke-filled room, holy shit guy I know hails from Croatia comes over tall chunky skin-head thick accent we shake hands like this, guy plays in punk band jean jacket long sideburns group of thugs beside him he's talking in my ear points to a table alright man I say, I take my friend over goth couple sitting there woman large round features death-white skin pierced nose black hair down to huge tits purple fingernails black lipstick guy looks just like her a bit taller sharper features she's wearing a dress I introduce everyone we hold court at middle table young punks constantly interrupting goth couple quite popular in here, my friend gets along with both easily exchanges wild stories lots of laughs we talk about music not much else telling me this quite the night,

"You see that tall chick with the cowboy hat?" says goth girl in my ear,

"Yeah"

"She's in the headlining band, they're fucking awesome"

"I see"

All drunk in this room what the hell else on draft night, goth guy drummer in the band been wanting to see his stuff for long time here we go hell for leather man, feel her hot breath on my ear goth lips moving up and down slightly words like whispers drown out everything, across the table my friend talking goth guy listening with serious intent he massages his Heineken gently she puts beer to her lips looks my way, The Jam starts playing in the background something from their first record synchronicity is everywhere improbable outcomes a daily occurrence drummer goes BBBBBBBOOMM, BATT-BAT, STATTU-STAT-CRASH even that happens with precise-awkward momentum go for it pal, you got nothing to lose few broken teeth not a big deal don't cry over lack of money power or women all means nothing equals circle represents integrity, goth guy telling his girl to fuck off she's giving it back they do this all the time part of their act looks serious (even they think it is) but it's not arms around each other in no time cuz they're what you call in love, human idealism, nothing else, but even that exists, go crazy, it's good for you...

Four of us cheering at nothing reporter friend a few
tables down I throw beer labels at him he returns the
favor beautiful young punk women circle the bar I stop
one know her from somewhere we talk laugh bullshit
she's wiry man got the juice running high girl beside
her talking to Croatian fellow making large sounds does
well with the women skin-head looking angry says
something to Croatian guy "fuck you" is his response
things back down but I sense trouble primal urge inside
us still running wild across the Savannas there's blood
on our chins every last one of us giraffe hooker orders
bar shots monkey man grunts strokes his mohawk
smoke so thick feel alive on death's corner waitress
lights joint passes it on moves with tray in one hand
enough drinks to feed battalion she's tough talk no
bullshit occasional laugh then back to face carved in
ivory liquor store man like lightning in your living room
stroke yourself rummy got a spot up in the trees just for
you skull bashed in blue-collar-hopeless it's after us no
time left order a drink bar owner looking drunk as the
rest greasy comb-over cigar in hand girl by mirrors
with pig-tails two drafts in small hands cigarette in

mouth lying softly guy with her swallows sad sight on the underbrush got no use for the world gone peaceful destructive gone mad time ticking guitar riff like Angus old girlfriend she crazy lives in a mansion greased-up butler sings St. Anthony's song "this is a song about a superhero named Tony" bad brain lover drives Jag through hills of Europe car crash blue intensity joker's running pool table awry dark back alley home to the sons of no one dignity gone hunting baby bullet wound through psyche unconscious ideas no longer walk in the park all quiet hear the church bells ring for thee granola monster thrashing up the place lost job manor lover gone Typhoid Mary cat-o-nine-tails skinning your ass cheeks stiletto down your throat ain't no time for despair go crazy man if needed just for awhile, everything is perfect, everything except for us and anything that comes from us, bumming smokes from goth girl she's serious film buff telling me about cinematographer on the movie Seven, then she's talking about Japanese movies in relation to Tarantino,

"That was obvious from the beginning" I say,

"See that guy? By the pool table?"

"Yeah"

"I fucked him in one of the rooms upstairs the other night"

"Kinda young, isn't he?"

"And hung like a horse"

Having good time here at this particular table my friend talking to goth guy easily known him for long time good fellow kind of shy actually, she's doing most of the talking aggressive loaded with laughing he's got long curly black hair leather pants good fellow I tell you, Croatian guy walks by large skin-head taunting him goth guy stands up Croatia guy being cool about whole thing unlike him normally blood would be drawn turns around skin-head hits him in back of the head with beer bottle thunks off his skull goth guy few others jump in whole bar notices my friend leans back I walk to the bar order a drink skin-head out on his ass Croatian guy holding bloodied cloth to back of head no sign of leaving he's got a beer owner hovering over him everyone laughing digging the sights all that's needed to stir things up is a bit of violence how we ever crawled down from the trees a mystery to me, young guys from band with cowboy girl come up to me say some thing in

my ear, I motion to my friend she walks over pendulum
hips moving from side to side,

"You want to go have a few drinks in the band room
with these guys?"

Before she answers girl with cowboy hat takes her
arm we start moving to the front lobby up the stairs
everything filthy green carpet pock-marked walls stinks
like piss and beer running up and down the hallways
like madmen old guy pokes his head out, we tell him to
go back to sleep it's our time mister, up two flights of
stairs enter room just like all other rooms in these
downtown fleabags bed no sheets stained mattress
broken-down chair in the corner, my friend comments
on the mattress I take a dive on it and kick back, beers
are passed around people come in a steady stream
young punk rockers some guys in their thirties guitar
playing happening by window it's a beautiful day in the
neighborhood, I'm talking to everyone who comes my
way always had more stamina than most my friend
doing the same thing across the room cowboy girl
listens intently then gives an order to one of her flunkies
few pills come out she pops them along with band
members no thanks I say, open window cold air rushing

in feels great my friend beside me arm brushing up against my side got my arm around her then I don't, we're drinking hard kicking back room rowdy young punks loud obnoxious feel like taking off but the veteran knows how to groove it kick back start talking shit rock and roll pizza pops and 7-11's, I'm laughing with young woman, younger than bus-stop-girl about old guy down the hall she's telling me some funny stories this guy fought in Korea apparently probably bullshit but one's story as good as the other the truth much cloudier than you think, several suburban punks in the room can always tell the difference the edge not quite there got no problem with them as lousy as anyone guy got crooked grin tougher than the rest he's got the crowd when he wants it we actually go back and forth for awhile me and him with the anecdotes I shake his hand good kid, washroom tiny and filthy I'm looking in the mirror not liking what I see yet strange confidence and attachment to myself have always enjoyed own company above all else, hanging out with people is alright too as long as mood's there and the booze flows, you're a scruff I say to my reflection, nothing but, walk out she's right here hugs me retreat to a corner and start kissing slowly tongues down each other's throats bashing teeth in this flophouse I grab her thigh been wanting to all fucking day feel the muscle surrounded by fat something happening in my jeans hand moves to her breast she's pressing up against me tongue is in my ear then we pull back look at each other bit of sadness in the air...

Got sudden memory of writing in my apartment hot summer nights in my underwear by windows on the 18th floor looking at Winnipeg skyline exchange district down below voices as clear as if they were right outside my window young punks in band ask me if I want to check out the roof, alright I say, I follow two guys down the hall see cockroach in doorway young woman on payphone tight shorts wool socks reach an open window at end of hallway follow me says guy we step out onto the fire escape, up the steel railways passing windows and people doing what they do in these places snow still falling slowly in big flakes reach a point where stairs end leading to a steel pipe leading to the roof...see first guy scramble up there no problem young fucker second guy begins,

"I'm not going up there boys" I say,

"Why, don't worry, it's easy look..."

Guy scrambles up like a drunken squirrel,

I laugh "I'll see you guys back in the room"

Make my way back down too drunk but still clearheaded enough to know those last couple of feet to the roof would have done me in got visions of broken body on pavement not interested in death, it's life I'm obsessed with, young punks must have thought I was soft I'll show those fuckers urban living calm down easy and quick realize it's not at all important, walking through hallways too familiar kinda depressing what the hell, should I move to the suburbs and mow the lawn every Sunday? On right landing see people coming in and out of the band-room make my way in first thing my friend hugs me takes my hand we sit and start talking...

People bitching about everything that's what we do, put us in paradise we will find something to complain about grass always greener have tried my entire life to focus on today and here not entirely possible don't want to talk about other places, not interested in the Eiffel Tower the Coliseum Mardi Gras or the Muslim churches of India, strongly believe in kindness and respect for everyone but don't piss me off man cuz treat me well you got a friend for life, friends a rare commodity, I say 'friends' not drinking buddies, you find the real thing hang on buddy, nothing better than a true friend keep in mind all things must end you'll be okay thunder clouds always present it's alright, twisted nipple in the torchlight ass like Saskatchewan in the moonlight, we've left the band-room on each floor there's a landing with a small couch and a window we're on the second floor wrestling on the couch bashing teeth again sloppy drunk she's got her hand between my legs rubbing and grinding my cock pushing at my jeans making small animal noises nothing graceful about sex we're a couple of monkeys banging it out in the jungle she's breathing hard tits in my hands got her crotch working and pulsing fall off the couch get back up again not much room clumsy struggle for territory she's moving her basketball ass side to side couple of people go by I'm aware of it and it bothers me,

"Don't worry" she says,

"Okay"

Kissing wild tasting the booze on her lips feel like doing nothing, going nowhere, rub your hand down her thigh and count your blessings, I'm up against the wall she's grinding her crotch into mine her tits flat against my chest somehow we stop continue slowly then stop again,

"To be continued" she smiles slurring just a touch enough to be sexy,

"I need a beer"

We walk back into the room find our way to a couple of beers everything right where we left it same faces same talk people generally predictable close to midnight what a fucking day confusing bar crawl wild woman like volcano-ash crawling up your legs she's tamed jungle meat if I allowed myself I could fall in love this instant, but it's been hell of a long time, best to play it cool son-of-a-bitch room starts to thin out decide it's time for the bar we walk the stairs again different parties in different rooms this slow-mo-survival herd gone crazy leader gone wild heavy metal rain over Torino Italy, here in The Peg six month winters incredibly hot summers bus-stop-girl got something to do with whole thing somehow she's holding my hand funny walk arms bigger than mine we both got a bit of the stumble cigarettes in our mouths on our way to meet things head-on reach the bar fucked-up scene crowded beyond enjoyment we slice right through it reach the bar get some drinks lean up against the wall I give my jacket to her to hold go outside for air stunning out here with the snow falling and the colors of The Exchange District few people scattered in front of the place as always stupid conversations try to block them out focus on the fire escapes small shops neon in the distance clock on top of city hall says 12:25 get your ass kicked it's okay, get dumped by your lover and laugh out loud, loose your job and say fuck it, none of it means shit just the falling snow and the cobblestone street going away from you, her face appears inside my head see her approach me at bus-stop, had I turned the other way I'd be at work feeling shitty with nothing but money security is the death of the artist, go back inside she's standing in corner as soon as I approach she thanks me and hits the dance floor see that idiot's cowboy hat towering above everything music blasting away feeling unafraid restless energy gone haywire reporter friend here once again hey man I shake his hand,

"Christ am I drunk" he says,

"Yeah..."

"No you don't get it, I'm drunk man"

Good guy intelligent lonely fucker have always gravitated to that type can almost hear the clock ticking in their lives in perfect rhythm with mine though my life not lonely at all have always been removed from society living on the fringe, find comfort in the ideas of the detached feel absolutely no pressure from present day morays stopped listening at very early age, product of parental divorce I was 15 wild completely out of control discovered sex drugs and rock and roll at precisely that time been a failure (as society would have it) ever since kept smiling however the smile of the happily detached, no problem gathering people around me have always formed micro sub-cultures without ever being conscious of it, suddenly there would be a gang around me this being before I started recognizing the reclusive tendencies under the surface had been there all along, spent childhood happy in dreamland collected comic books beginning of my artistic life feel like a child still

at this very moment, reporter saying something I've got
him completely blocked out stupid grin on my face
mind wandering through different stages of my life it's
been quite the trip taught myself how to play guitar,
published underground writer of poems and novels,
been kicked around plenty bad times with bad women
suicide friends, sold grass for a living for many years
(should get back into that), dishwasher, university
student, welfare bum, bar-crawling for twenty years
I'm traveling back in time, back and forth at will
groovy trip the grown-ups would have said in my
childhood raised in Fort Rouge (little Italy) lower
working-class neighborhood small houses large trees
lined the streets forming a canopy over them shading
the sidewalks for those hot fucking Winnipeg summers
the smell of green grass everywhere I'm sitting in the
park on the swings reading a Spiderman comic, little
Italian friend lives in brown duplex likes DC comics
better than Marvel, Earl Grey school across the street
from my house on corner of Garwood and Arbuthnot,
had friends of all races East Indian, Aboriginal, Asian,
couple of black kids lived on the other corner had crush
on their sister, Italians were everywhere souped-up

Camaros and Trans-Ams Corvettes and Mustangs burning rubber driving the parents crazy, what a trip, I'm in Italy living in a villa up in the hills the Italian Alps in the distance, I'm grabbing a peach from one of the trees in our backyard, Fiorenza is there in a red one-piece bathing suit, we're wrestling around in the backyard I'm feeling her thighs rubbing against me, we're talking in my room got my old Kiss records on, I'm on stage the guitar licks shooting out the end of my guitar there are three people in the entire room one of them is my girlfriend, to be alive is to live in character and to wonder what put things in motion, how much of it was you and how much was that other thing...

Reporter slurring his words to me,
"Know what I mean?" he says,
"What's that?"
"I said, know what I mean?"
"Sure, I know, I know, don't worry it'll be okay"
Couple of hippies in room stand out horribly and I mean hippies not regular long-hairs like me they have the clothes and the beads look uncomfortable about to

leave, better to leave soon few skin-heads in room nasty looking for a taste of blood, hippies out the door I'm glad for them don't like their philosophy but don't want to see them hurt, peace is a good thing but it's not the only thing, she's back caressing my shoulder looking me right in the eye mischievous smile on her face can't keep hands off of each other leaning up against pinball machine in the thick cigarette smoke smell of booze goes right up your nostrils I'm kissing her earlobe she's giggling wildly electric shock down your trousers up to your neck in questions her knee keeps tapping my cock, tap, tap tap, tap, one hand on her waist I'm moving other up and down her ass in slow motion following the curve never felt anything so perfectly round no shit feels like I'm rubbing a basketball, I'm completely entranced by this expression of pure sex going up and down, up, down, big old ass...

"Did I tell you" she says in my ear "my mother's black"

"Ahh, that explains it"

She giggles,

"Black people have the nicest asses in the world"

"No argument" I say,

"Tell me how round it is"

"It's as round as a cannonball, uhhh..."

"Again"

"You could serve drinks on this ass"

"No doubt sugar-daddy"

Loud laughter beside us Croatian fellow hanging tough with buddies got headband on minor distraction in the bar-light my hand feeling that leg move forward always been a leg man brain starting to salivate she got big long thighs heavy and sensual quite the buxom Native girl African blood flowing through her veins adding curves to her body wonder if she paints her toes bodies close drinking still always drinking we light cigarettes and taste each other's tongues blow smoke in the air not searching for enlightenment or anything of that nature just this room and all the punks in it, certain people I know see me keep moving like it's understood the moment doesn't include them greasy hamburger at corner diner smothered in gravy and fried onions by the lake cold beer in hand cigarette almost finished water winding itself around thick green forest cement under my footsteps neon drunk crazy lesbian hair like Toronado whorehouse on corner city skyline lit up like war zone fireworks over the horizon visible from my window skyscrapers neon colors red, blue, green, yellow night is blinding, see here I say to my friend,

"This is a fucked-up reality"

"Sure, but it's not my fault, I promise" she says eyes elsewhere,

Owner sitting at back of the bar large smile on face raking in the dough tonight lit cigar in hand kind with tips on the end someone on stage I think not planned unrehearsed most of it shit some funny parts small wiry guy alone with Strat loud distorted songs about nothing (that's the good part) seems to get quite a rise from this collection of absurd alcoholics bizarre state of mind she leans against the wall for first time today I see wasted eyes body slumping, I give her room and the privacy she deserves most important thing in life I spend four or five days out of seven alone digging every moment of it entirely by choice know enough people to party every night but not into that groove have to write cuz any fool can party all night myself included getting high still favorite pastime can't stop smoking lighting one after the other nicotine junky there are worse kinds talking to some guy by the men's washroom about something he's friendly I return the favor alright he says and splits, she comes up to me says she's going dancing with this guy over here friend of her's, okay man, not a problem, got her second wind I'm impressed lazy-walk to the bar more room here now most punks at the front slowly order a drink bartender full of sweat he's handing me the glass, I'm paying him, I'm refusing change, there's a small black dot in my Rye and 7, I'm tipping the glass to my mouth everything feels slow then sudden increase in speed reality comes rushing through my brain in waves of red and black I drain half the glass put it down grab a smoke,

"No more smoking in bars next week" says the bartender as he lights my smoke,

Say nothing keep moving rapid-fire sensation in tune with entire face giant no mystery to us bastards in the sun she's crocodile dizzy right out the window, I can see that big head of hair bopping up and down to DOA thick curls lashing around like a whip, no adventure is necessary my man, pull back hard and tight relentless in your pursuit of non-performance, psyche in high gear confident and alive purple rainbows excuse me while I tie my shoelace fucking thing snaps with no time left bus-driver corrupt manic depressive mutilated organ tissue laughing my head off with reporter friend I'm increasingly impressed with this man, make note to seek him out more often very rare thing for me to do not easily surprised by people he's telling me about Younge Street in Toronto sounds exciting alive and electric very little of that in this town without the drunken violence, he prefers it there but too expensive man,

"Figure I'll stay here and drink myself to an early grave"

"Not necessarily, you can drink till a ripe old age if you know how to do it"

"Christ man, and how the fuck is that?"

"As long as you're in charge, not the bottle"

Walk away to edge of dance floor is full no mosh-pit but body grinding against body, slow-motion-girl sees me shakes her ass giving me the peace sign I laugh beautiful sight people dressed in black everywhere mohawks jutting upwards like spikes of multi-colored steel fight by elevator soft-ass thing guys too drunk for anything acting macho-shithead cuz there's a couple of chicks hanging around, wish that behavior could be eliminated in men never understood it, never will, you could have four college professors in a room with three phd's a head and if they're all men the infantile competition will begin IQ level will drop dramatically, it's back to high school man, I hated it then I hate it even more now, men are no damn good, short guy with glasses bald head starts talking to me can't make out a fucking word he's saying getting on my nerves very quickly I move away with a smile guy gets the point everyone waiting for last band of the night taking their sweet time in typical rock star fashion cowboy girl and her flunkies somewhere getting wasted maybe they're gone for the night, backed up a band once who never showed we ended up playing entire night repeating songs cuz we didn't have enough material not good night but we didn't give a shit, she's with me again, we're holding each other happy and sad, saying something in my ear smiling like a tomcat killer grizzly sexy and wild take off your head man, I know, I'm telling her, I know, I find being with a woman to be very strange, I'm alone most of the time feeling alive in tune electric then there's a woman things feel good but rhythm out of whack strange sensations thoughts in your head suddenly reflection in mirror looks different and it goes like this for awhile then alone again at first feeling shitty and depressed then groove comes back I'm walking to the right beat getting laid once in awhile (would like more of that) drinking beer under an umbrella living breathing walking the streets and writing about it, yet the drive to seek out mates undeniable the right woman can stretch out your life in the strangest of ways, the wrong woman say hello to an early grave, best to be alone she says, don't think she knows I heard that I can feel her moving away from me even with her arms around me another guy asks her to dance she says no,

"You wouldn't dance with me, would you?"

"No, aah, not very good at it..."

"It's okay...really, it's okay...I have to talk to you" she says with a smile,

"Juicy"

"I'm serious..."

"Alright, go ahead"

"Not now...I've been conflicted all night...after the show, okay?"

"No problem"

Big smile I take her hand we move upstairs to the second landing we're on a couch kissing like animals sloppy and wet booze coming out every pore hand on her crotch rubbing softly then harder she's moaning moaning sounds like a Lou Reed song I'm lying on top of her our jeans grinding into each other she's biting my neck her teeth pulling at my beard "ugggg" roll off the couch on the ground she's on top things seem to speed up we're like a couple of sand lizards writhing in the moonlight fighting staking our territory this the silent war baby someone walks by don't give it a notice she's rubbing her tits all over me body going up and down side to side start unbuttoning her pants goddamit hear the owner's voice coming up the stairs for fuck's sake my friend gets up we sit on the couch watch him walk by pissed off as hell his son hangs out with us,

"Good night, ey?" he says,

"Sure" I say,

We say nothing for a few minutes,

"Fucking hot down there" he says,

She takes my hand with anger we're moving down the stairs I wrench my hand away "take it easy baby, alright?" she looks into me, I take it unafraid, she ends up turning away first, "we gotta talk" she says as she goes down the stairs her ass jiggling away from me...

On the dance floor again she looks at me every few seconds winking smiling her partner's one of those young punkers from outside I watch her move one last time her hips shaking my head feel touch of sadness, one last time bright red lips go "yeah!", one last time green wolf eyes on mine asking questions, one last time I drain my glass watch her move deeper into the dance floor she's laughing so beautiful her legs far away now in the darkness I can feel her breath on my neck, so beautiful, I move out the door into the winter night and start moving down the sidewalk snow continues to fall in gigantic far-apart flakes the beauty of this night palpable, icicles hang from awnings like crystal diamonds drops of water roll down their sides, really warm out here leather jacket unzipped light a smoke got my head up walking fairly straight slow and low-down ice melting on the street forms puddles step up and around deep red puffs of smoke in my lungs there's a street juggler in front of arched tunnel eyes like fire smiles as I walk by reach the end of street look back and he's gone, thin mist hovers in the air walk through it into the night feel sad but free in the understanding all emotions must be experienced to be alive, another tunnel pitch black I'm inside it not very long cobblestone street garbage everywhere mist at the entrance time to move on out into the street follow the sidewalk and the streetlights feel thirsty take a chunk of snow and taste it got visions of this very street in summer leaves on the small trees lights everywhere people hanging around smoking cigarettes sitting on the benches just three months away and it's a different world get away from downtown this city feels like an urban forest in summer there's so much green it can strangle you, cut through a back alley then a parking lot there's a church on the corner, across the street there's a whorehouse, fire station two blocks down damn sirens wailing every twenty minutes man, there goes one now pretty close unable to see exactly what's going on hookers indoors cops drinking whiskey firefighters do the rumba I'm approaching home...gut uneasy feel the air as I spin in it lean up against the church see a bright red smile in my head makes me think and maybe feel the sadness absurdity of living smoky hallway martini glass ambiguous lecher laughs in your sleep illusions are everywhere no time for fear induced argument unconscious mind leads the way what's the point she says, I want to sing like Tom Waits I say tuning the guitar smoking cigs how's that I say, sounds groovy she says groovy like T. Rex, mind tries to fast forward to tomorrow I stop it dead in its tracks no time for tomorrow sister says Taoist Charley, you can kiss my ass she says with all the other religions running wild fucking up everything take a seat on a snow bank and look around, not a soul in sight things so quiet they're almost maddening in the distance feint sound of cars going somewhere but that's about all dead and waiting everything in transition waiting for that one fucking thing to wake them up from living eyes shut mind whiskey-gnarled thinking about old friend ex-con from old neighborhood laughing with him in the unemployment office last year meeting over we're in Central Park smoking a joint talking about how much we hate work, once again feeling that bit of fear every jobless person feels, how long till my luck runs out? How much time do I got? Can I lazy about one more night? Fight it off those thoughts no damn good to anyone start moving again light another smoke walk right by whorehouse feel tremendous urge to walk through front door got no money of course so what the fuck, reach my building group of Arabs there women in traditional head-scarves "hello" I say, they return the favor very friendly enjoying the break in the weather I see more people around the corner by the Mac's store attached to building black guys hang out there day and night just leaning back smoking cigarettes always speaking in their African tongues know a few of them we start kind of talking on street corner even more people out on Q'uappelle Street by Central Park everyone digging the winter-night the drunks are out hint of violence always in the air but not a problem get your ass out on the street man just for a second check it out dig the sounds see my neighbor cutting through the park he's got jug of beer in hand hey he says, hands me a swig I take it give it back, what's up with your girlfriend I say, no more girlfriend he says, take a swig, we pass it back and forth, do you believe in God he says, I'll see you later man I say, turn the corner Chinese fellow asks me for cigarette I give him one drunken

Native woman very tall rough sexy propositions people well known small-time whore walk right by her inside the store smell coffee and donuts thinking this is alright black guy behind counter few people scattered around the place take the door to the hallway leads to main lobby of my building press for the elevator two Arabs a black woman three Native guys and me get into the elevator damn machine takes its time all of us uncomfortable I finally get to the 18th floor down the hall into my apartment it's dirty scattered books and magazines on the floor beer cans on kitchen counter (grab a full one from the fridge) half empty bag of weed empty cigarette packs on coffee-table roaches in the ashtray smells like booze in here go to my huge windows open them up downtown skyline in front of me and the streets of the exchange district that we've been walking all day and night, me and her, couple guys are getting into it in front of a building, few punches are thrown, voices sound like they're right in my living-room something about a chick and some beer, one guy takes off other follows down the street so young and fast man moving full speed through a parking lot they disappear round the corner, I sit on the couch feel something in my pockets reach in there, it's the gram of hash, my friend's gift to me for a moment unplanned, I see her right now standing here in cherry red underwear, I'm reaching forward touching her thighs, she's on my lap we're kissing, she's beside me on the couch we're smoking a joint and talking and listening to The Pixies, her fingernails are painted blue as are her toes, we're walking down the street her smile directed at me, we're in a drugstore her tears fall down in slow motion, lost my job for her would do it all over again, I look over to the answering machine expecting to hear message that I was fired, light unblinking I check again, not a single message, what a monumental joke man, what an abomination, I feel like crying but nothing comes out cuz it all turns out madly in the end and I met a girl at a bus-stop today, what a blast it was to know her...

Tony Nesca was born in Torino, Italy in 1965 and moved to Canada at the age of three. He was raised in Winnipeg but relocated back to Italy several times until finally settling in Winnipeg in 1980. He taught himself how to play guitar and formed an original rock band playing the local bars for several years. At the age of twenty-seven he traded his guitar for a Commodore 64 and started writing seriously. He has published six chapbooks of stories and poems (which he used to sell straight out of his knapsack at local dives and bookstores), six novels, four books of poetry, one short story collection, and has been an active contributor to the underground lit scene for fifteen years, being published in innumerable magazines both online and in print. He currently resides in Winnipeg.

Screamin' Skull Press

Cutting Edge
Spontaneous
Street-Writing

Novels, Stories, Poems

Tony Nesca   Nicole I. Nesca